Cavas

The Vorge Crew – Book Five

By Laurann Dohner

Cavas by Laurann Dohner

Career military man Cavas Vellar has joined his older brother, Cathian, aboard The Vorge for one purpose—to rescue their youngest littermate. Their father has resorted to having him kidnapped to hide one of his most vile secrets. They need to go down onto a planet full of criminals, find Crath, and rescue him. This mission is the most important one Cavas has ever led.

Jill was betrayed when Earth sold her into alien slavery. She owes her life to Cavas and the *Vorge* crew for taking her out of a cell and to their ship. When she learns why they were on that planet to begin with…she feels it's her duty to help them find their missing brother. Even if it means losing her recently gained freedom.

One determined alien on a mission. One woman who notices how sexy he is. This is their story.

The Vorge Crew Series List

Cathian

Dovis

York

Raff

Cavas

Cavas by Laurann Dohner

Editor: Kelli Collins

Cover Art: Dar Albert

ISBN: 978-1-950597-09-3

Cavas – The Vorge Crew – Book Five

By Laurann Dohner

Chapter One

Cavas took in *The Vorge* crew members as he entered the dining hall. He'd gotten a debriefing on each one of them from Marrow before they'd exchanged places.

Every face he glanced at showed surprise, except for those of the three Pod aliens. The small beings were a telepathic race with strong mind-reading abilities. He'd been talking to them by broadcasting his thoughts since the moment he'd boarded the vessel, asking for their silence. It seemed they'd heeded his request.

Cathian, his older brother by one minute, rose to his feet. "Cavas!"

"It's good to see you. I'm sorry for the early-morning shock."

Cathian lunged forward and opened his arms, hugging him tight. Cavas chuckled, giving his brother a bracing squeeze back.

They parted. Cathian stared intently into his eyes. "What's going on?"

He hesitated in answering. "I need you to remain calm." Cavas stepped back, making eye contact with each of the crew present. "I need *all* of you to remain calm."

"Cavas..." Cathian reached out and gripped his arm. He wore a confused expression.

"I think it's best if you and Raff come with me to have a private discussion. This is a family matter."

Raff lifted a small female with black hair off his lap and rose. It had to be his life-lock, Lilly. Cavas had heard about her...and how his father hadn't been pleased with their cousin finding a human.

Cathian released Cavas and motioned for Raff to halt. He scowled. "We don't keep secrets from each other. Tell us why you are here. How did you even get onboard without us being alerted?"

"Marrow helped me," Cavas admitted.

Cathian glanced around. "Where is she?" He started to reach for his ship com to call her.

Cavas stayed his hand by gripping his wrist. "She won't answer. Currently, she's on the shuttle I arrived in, on her way to Rave station."

A snarl ripped from his older brother. "She's not military! You gave her orders? I won't allow you to use *The Vorge* for one of your operations. It's not happening. We have females now. One of them is pregnant!"

"Calm," Cavas snarled back. "I resigned from the military, Cathian. I'm not taking over your vessel or your crew. I asked Marrow for a *favor*. She agreed after I told her what was happening. She shouldn't be in any danger. Just hear me out."

The rage eased from Cathian's face, surprise taking its place. "You resigned? You live for the Tryleskian military. It's who you are."

"Not anymore. We really should have this discussion in private."

Raff came forward.

Cavas tensed, prepared to defend himself against an attack from his cousin. He had learned everything he could about Raff once he'd become aware of his existence. He respected Raff for surviving all that he had...but his cousin was an efficient killer. Cavas would be stupid to forget that.

Raff halted a few feet away, studying him from head to foot.

"I'm no threat to you," Cavas assured him. "You're partially why I resigned. I want that clear before we speak. I was outraged when I heard what our fathers did to you. You have my loyalty above them. My word." He tapped his chest, holding Raff's gaze. It was a silent vow of loyalty and honesty. "We *are* family."

Raff gave a sharp nod.

Cathian's shoulders sagged. "What has Father done now?"

It was Cavas's turn to be surprised. "I thought I'd have to convince you to believe me when I tell you he's done something dishonorable."

"I deal with Father often. Also, you quit the military and snuck aboard my ship. You wouldn't do either unless he'd done something terrible, and it probably somehow involves Raff, the person he currently hates most. Tell us everything."

Cavas kept most of his focus on Raff. That's where the threat lie. "I was ordered to pick five of my most trusted soldiers, fly here to board *The Vorge* by force, and arrest Raff. Then I was to personally interrogate him, using whatever torture necessary, to retrieve unknown documents from him that could harm our family name. After that, my orders were to dispose of his body. I refused."

Raff didn't show a hint of expression or move but he did blink a few times. Then a cold smile curved his lips. "I would have killed all six of you."

8

"We're blood," Cavas reminded him. "I would *never* follow those orders." He touched his chest again. He turned his attention to Cathian. "Father wasn't pleased when I told him no. I also pointed out that he's made many enemies in the military, so if he sent another team, they'd use any documentation they obtained to destroy him. I'd thought I was very convincing. Six days later, he showed up on my ship to have a private word with me."

Rage almost choked Cavas as he remembered that conversation. He took a calming breath. "He said if I ever wanted to see Crath again, I'd assemble that team and do my duty to protect the Vellar name. He was counting on my bond to our youngest littermate being stronger than that with my cousin."

Cathian paled.

"I immediately reached out to Crath. I couldn't locate him. He's missing, Cathian. Father has done something to him.

"I immediately resigned and fled Tryleskian airspace. I flew my private shuttle to Rave station, took on a false identity, and bought another shuttle. I came here right after. No one knows that but Marrow, and now the people in this room. Marrow is going to pick up my shuttle and lead Father on a false trail. I'm sure he's tracking it. We need to go find Crath before Father realizes I'm looking for him. He was last seen on Flax Colony."

Cathian threw back his head and roared in rage.

Cavas understood; he had already done that a few times now. He turned his focus to Raff. "We're going to need your skills, cousin. Flax is run by Yorlian Trevis. He's a Tryleskian who bought the planet twenty years ago. He has childhood ties to both of our fathers and is a known criminal. If Crath was on Flax, Trevis could easily snatch him, holding him as a favor to my father."

"I'm going to kill our father," Cathian snarled.

Cavas gave a nod, not surprised. "I wanted to snap his neck as he stood before me threatening our youngest littermate, but I refrained. Crath will stay alive as long as our father believes that he can use him against me. Right now, he probably figures I'm taking advantage of the bars and pleasure houses that make Rave station popular. I also had Marrow take some of your systems offline to prevent him from finding out I've joined forces with you and your crew. He might be monitoring your main computer, Cathian."

"I'm in," Raff growled.

Cavas wasn't surprised. "Thank you."

Dovis and York came forward to join them. "We're all in," Dovis said.

Cathian nodded. "We're going to get our brother." He turned, gesturing to a long-haired human female. "Mari, I know I usually ask you to keep things in great working order...but get rid of our transponder, shut down all exterior communications, and tear out anything that will help us be tracked. Shut down anything you need to, even if we go all manual." He pointed at York. "Change course once she's done. You heard where we're going." Then to Dovis, "Start preparing for battle. Make sure every weapon is charged and ready to use."

The three of them rushed from the dining hall to carry out his orders.

Cavas reached out and touched his brother's chest. "We'll get Crath back. We're always strongest together."

Cathian gripped his hand, the touch helping their bond reconnect. "Always."

* * * * *

During his research, Cavas had learned Yorlian Trevis had committed crimes ranging from murder to kidnapping for ransom to illegal slave ownership. He'd even been brought to trial, and should have received life in prison, or even execution. Instead, a wealthy family on the Tryleskian home world had intervened, then he'd been banished from ever returning to the planet.

It had pissed Cavas off when he'd learned his father and uncle were the wealthy Tryleskians who'd aided Trevis.

The criminal had fled and bought Flax, a small dirt planet far from the Tryleskian home world, where Cavas had just landed *The Vorge's* shuttle. They'd painted it with a new name to hide the shuttle's identity.

Flax colony was the only existing city on the planet. It was loud, overcrowded, and had become a haven for outlaws.

Cavas adjusted his tinted goggles that hid his eyes and part of his face, reaching up to shove his dark blonde hair out of the way. It annoyed him, but a nearly shaved head indicated he was military. The medical android on *The Vorge* had helped him rapidly grow it a bit, injecting simulation shots into his scalp. He wasn't used to having a mane.

The male on his left looked equally uncomfortable. Dovis usually traveled in his furry form. To avoid them being recognized, the shapeshifter had stayed in skin. Another growl tore from the male's throat as he adjusted the loose sleeves over his arms.

"I understand," Cavas muttered. "I hate their clothing, too. They wear them four times too large. And I'm already sick of the dust flying around here."

"Why do they dress this way?"

Cavas hid his amusement over how annoyed Dovis sounded. "They think it will keep all the dust from getting inside their clothing and becoming trapped. I never said the people who live here were smart...but we need to fit in."

"I hope the others are having better luck than we are."

They'd separated into two teams when they'd landed on the surface. Cavas had paired up with Dovis. Cathian stuck with their cousin Raff. York had stayed on the ship in orbit to protect all the females, in case *The Vorge* was attacked. He'd been chosen because his mate was pregnant, and Cavas had easily agreed. The Parri male might be an excellent fighter but he had a family to think about.

Cavas understood the need to protect family. His younger brother by two minutes was being held against his will.

They needed to find and rescue Crath.

Life sign scans hadn't helped locate him. They also hadn't been able to bring down one of the Pods to scan for his littermate's thoughts. Pods were valuable on the black market. There were over three hundred Tryleskian males on the surface, and few with integrity would work for someone like Yorlian Trevis. Pods would be too tempting to steal on a planet of thieves.

That left the four of them walking aimlessly around the colony, searching for information on their own.

They entered Yorlian Trevis's favorite bar—which he owned—taking seats on opposite ends of the long counter. Rumors implied there were hidden holding cell somewhere on the premises.

Cavas ordered the strongest drink they served. All his years in the military gave him an advantage. It had become almost impossible for him to get drunk.

He hid a smile, thinking of the friends he'd grown close to who loved to buy drinks for their superior officer, trying to get him wasted, to no avail.

Anger followed. That life had been taken from him. He could never return to military service for his planet. His father had made certain of that.

A green female approached him. He couldn't identify her race, but he recognized traits from a few. She was probably a blend of many. It was common for multi-species breeding on outlaw colony planets. He'd visited several of them over the years.

The woman took a seat and flashed her orange teeth. "Buy me a drink?"

"Sure." He motioned to the bartender, who hustled over, as if expecting it.

Cavas made note of that.

"What's your name? I haven't seen you here before." Her light, flirty tone belied the sharpness in her yellow eyes.

"Jorgan." He had false identity to back up the name. "You?"

"Pree. What brings you here?"

He lifted his drink. "To get drunk."

She laughed, the braying sound grating on his nerves. "I meant to our little colony."

"I'm between jobs and seeking work." He let his gaze trail over her body, playing his part. "Do you know anyone hiring?"

"It depends on what you do."

"Anything that pays well." He shrugged, taking another sip.

She accepted her drink. "Looking for some fun in the meantime? I'm available for a price."

Cavas took in the details of her dress, the flashy jewelry she wore, and his suspicion piqued. She looked too high-quality for a dive bar.

Out of the corner of his eye, he spotted two bouncers inching closer.

She worked there, all right, but Cavas didn't think it was for sex. He'd been in situations like this before. She was testing him.

He'd play along. "How much? I have to watch my creds."

"A hundred...but nothing violent."

He forced a smile. "That sounds good. Do you have a place nearby we could go? I doubt you want to follow me all the way to my shuttle, but I'm game if you are. I really want to see you out of that dress."

She downed the contents of her glass. "You know what? I forgot I need to be somewhere." She speared a barely noticeable glance at the bartender, shaking her head subtly. The woman strolled toward the other end of the bar.

Cavas sipped his drink, having assured the female he wasn't an undercover authority. If he were, he'd have arrested her for propositioning him, or at least turned her down flat.

The bartender approached, wiping at the counter.

"I overheard what you said. I might know of a job."

He sat up straighter. "I would appreciate it." It might help him gain information, especially if he were to work directly for Yorlian Trevis. Everyone on the colony seemed to in one way or another.

"What did you do before?"

"This and that."

"You're not very talkative."

"It pays to keep my mouth shut. I like creds more than conversation."

The bartender nodded. "Let me talk to someone. I'll be back."

He noticed that Pree had strode up to Dovis, who was rapidly shaking his head. Cavas wanted to groan. The male was mated, of course he'd instantly say no to sex. Amarains like Dovis bonded to one female for life.

The response was swift. One moment Dovis sat on the barstool, and the next, the two bouncers were on him.

Cavas remained still, torn between helping him and keeping his cover. He needn't have worried. The head of security for *The Vorge* was a good fighter, even in skin. Dovis took down both bouncers fast, standing over their unconscious bodies in seconds.

The bartender jumped over the counter and tried to take him down next. Dovis turned and punched him in the face. The sound of bones breaking was loud.

15

Cavas slid off his seat and leapt forward.

Dovis spun, fists raised, and snarled at Cavas.

He lifted his hands. "You just took out someone who might get me a job. Leave or I'll knock you out, *stranger*."

Dovis frowned momentarily—then attacked. Cavas dodged his fist easily and swung, pulling his own punch at the last second.

Dovis yelled out as if in pain and flew backward though, playing along. He crashed into the bar before sinking to his ass, pretending to be down for the count.

It was tough not to laugh. Cavas liked Cathian's crew. They would have made excellent soldiers. He stepped over Dovis's legs and helped the bartender up. Blood poured from his broken nose.

"Are you good?"

The bartender glanced at the unconscious bouncers, then at Dovis, still pretending to be unconscious. "You're hired. Pick that traitor up and carry him downstairs. We have holding cells."

Cavas gave a sharp nod. Dovis might not have meant to cause a fight but it had worked in their favor. "What's the pay?"

The bartender held his gaze. "Three hundred a day. Free room upstairs included, and two meals."

Cavas nodded and leaned down, grabbing hold of Dovis and hoisting him over his shoulder. The male kept his body lax. The bartender led him to the back of the bar and through one wide door before pointing out another. "Go down. Tell the guard that Mall sent you, and you're new. His name is Grah."

Cavas realized the second door didn't hide stairs, but a lift instead. He entered, glancing around stealthily, but there were no signs of security measures to monitor them. He shifted Dovis's limp body to a more comfortable position over his shoulder after the door sealed. "You weigh a ton," he whispered.

"You punch like a child."

Cavas fought a laugh and pushed the old-fashioned button to make the lift go down. "Interesting that they have a floor underground. Wouldn't it be great if Crath is down here?"

"We can't be lucky enough to find him *that* fast. They wouldn't make it too easy for us."

"I know. I just want to find him." The doors opened and Cavas stepped out.

A large red male with horns stood from his chair, reaching for the gun strapped to his hip. Dolten aliens were dumb creatures, mostly known for hiring out their muscle to others and eating uncooked meat. They were strong, though, and excellent fighters.

"Mall sent me. I'm Jorgan. You're Grah. I'm supposed to lock this one up. Mall said he's a traitor. Did he work here before or something?"

The guard took his hand off his weapon and came closer, his black eyes scanning Dovis. "No. Never smelled him before. Probably law. That's what we call them. They come here sometimes. We make them disappear. Good eating." He turned, walked to a solid metal wall, and pressed his hand against a reader pad nearby. "Follow me."

Cavas's humor had faded as the alien talked. They *ate* law enforcement? It sent a shiver down his spine. What kind of planet was Yorlian Trevis running?

A far worse one than they had imagined, if he allowed his hired thugs to eat prisoners.

Cavas followed the large alien into a mostly lit corridor with a long line of cells. The three they passed contained various aliens. Grah pulled his weapon, pointing it at the two occupants of the barred cell he stopped in front of, and waved his other wrist over the lock. The door slid open.

"Toss him in there."

Cavas tapped Dovis's leg to warn him. He couldn't see all the cells farther down, but he hoped Crath would be in one of them. But no way would he allow Dovis to be locked up—especially after the eating comment. "Sure thing. Just make sure you don't accidently shoot me. That's no stunner."

"Right. Mine makes big holes in prisoners if they rush me." Grah moved to the side, keeping his weapon pointed at the two males in the cell.

Cavas tensed as he stepped closer and gave three light taps in rapid succession for Dovis. His men knew what that meant, but he hoped the Amarian figured it out.

He reached the open cell—and suddenly twisted, dumping Dovis off his shoulder and lunging for the gun.

He grabbed the red alien's wrist and shoved it upward. The gun discharged into the ceiling, chunks of debris falling around them. Pieces of it hit Cavas but he barely noticed. He was too focused on the guard.

The bigger male recovered from the sudden attack and tried to use his clawed fingers to tear at Cavas's eyes. But Dovis was there, grabbing the red hand heading for his face and preventing it from doing damage. It took them both to steal his weapon and use it.

Grah wouldn't be eating any more prisoners ever again.

Cavas turned to study the two males inside the cell. They were against the back wall, watching with leery expressions, but they didn't try to escape through the open door. He pointed the weapon at the skinny blue alien he couldn't identify. "What are you in for?"

"Being the wrong skin color."

Cavas arched an eyebrow.

"Truth," the alien swore. "They hate blue skin here."

The yellow alien nodded. "They do. I'm here for not paying a bill— but they charged me four times for the same night. Nobody would listen to me."

"Have you seen a Tryleskian my size? Longer hair, black? He's probably going by the name of Brit?"

They both shook their heads.

"Stay put. We're releasing everyone soon, but I'm checking the other cells first. We stand a better chance of escaping if we all rush out of here together. Understood?"

The blue one wrung his long, skinny hands. "Truth?"

"Truth. Just stay put for now while we search. Then we'll leave. Everyone goes."

The yellow alien pushed off from the wall. "Don't release the green beast! Leave him."

Cavas frowned. "Why?"

The yellow alien shuddered. "He kills anyone they put in with him. Crazy. No control. He'll attack us all."

"I'll be careful."

Leaving Dovis at the open cell, Cavas moved to the next, peering in. Three prisoners were in the small space, all staring at him with hope. He guessed they'd overheard his conversation. Crath wasn't amongst them.

"Did you see—"

"No. Your kind *run* this planet. They don't get locked up," one of them said before he could finish.

Cavas moved on, peering inside each cell and asking about his brother. No one had any information to share. So far, all he'd learned was that Yorlian Trevis must have hired every dishonorable Tryleskian he could find.

Seven cells down, a Parri male stood holding on to the bars of the door. Cavas kept out of reach.

"I've seen Brit."

Cavas wanted to believe him. Most Parri were honorable. "When? Where? What do you know of him?"

The Parri hesitated. "You're letting us all out? I didn't do anything but visit. They grabbed me in the bar and brought me down here. Been here for a long time. Over a week. Maybe ten or eleven days. They *do* hate blue-skinned aliens here."

"We're letting everyone out but the green whatever he is. I'll toss him a weapon as we go. He can free himself after we're gone."

"Lost in rage," the Parri muttered. "They torture him when they get bored by shooting at him with electric sticks."

The news sickened Cavas but didn't surprise him. "Tell me about Brit."

The male pressed his face against the bars. "His eyes are blue, and he's got a scar on his neck. Left side."

Excitement filled Cavas. It sounded like his youngest littermate. Brit was the name he used when on questionable planets, to avoid someone attempting to ransom him as a Vellar. Crath had gained his scar three years before when someone had tried to grab him for that very purpose. And Flax had a lot of Tryleskians living there who'd easily identify their wealthy family name.

"Tell me everything."

"I met Brit the first night I was here, in another bar. He likes to drink and have a good time. Big on telling jokes and laughing. He also likes to fight."

That sounded like Crath. "What else can you tell me? He went missing. Do you know anything about that?"

"Sure do. We were drinking when a large group of security came looking for him. I don't know why. He seemed confused, too. I tried to help him get away, along with Kneello. They pulled out stunners and got all three of us. I woke up here."

Cavas wanted to snarl. "They didn't bring Brit here with you?"

"No. Kneello was. They took him away a few days ago. I heard one of the guards say it was to fight in the pits. He warned me that my turn would be coming soon."

"The pits?"

The Parri gave a grim nod. "I didn't believe it until they dragged Kneello out of here. Word is, they're illegal fights. I'm not rich enough to see them, nor am I into blood sport. A Crippon told me anyone who pissed off the owner of the colony disappears and ends up having to fight—to the death."

Cavas tried to remain calm. Trevis would want to keep Crath alive if he didn't want to piss off Beltsen Vellar. It was probably why his younger littermate wasn't in the holding cells under the bar with guards who tended to eat prisoners. "Thank you for the information."

He moved to another cell. The enraged green alien he'd heard about snarled at him, pacing the cell. He was a big creature of a few alien races, by the look of him, and the damage to his body made Cavas flinch. The guards had done a number on him.

"We're all getting out. Can you calm enough to talk to me?"

The green beast snarled and lunged. He hit the bars and reached through, trying to claw at him. Cavas leapt back, narrowly avoiding being hit.

"I guess that would be a no."

The next cell stood empty, and all the lights were turned off in the last six cells. He almost returned to Dovis before hesitating, wanting to make certain they'd left no males behind. He removed his goggles and went to the next one, allowing his eyes to adjust to the dark. It stood empty. So did the next two.

The fourth one, though, had a small form on the floor.

"Wake," he ordered. "Have you seen a Tryleskian named Brit?"

The form didn't move. It was covered in a blanket, and the smell of unwashed male bodies was the only thing he could pick up. It made him regret breathing deeply.

"They brought her in sick a few days ago," the Parri called out.

Her?

All the other prisoners had been male.

He used the bracelet he'd stolen off the dead guard and waved it at the door, unlocking it. The metal slid to the side. He stepped into the cell, prepared for an attack, but the form on the floor didn't stir.

Cavas crouched and lifted the blanket slightly, shocked by what he saw.

She was human. Cathian and his crew had mated to a few of them, and he could easily identify them by their tiny curved ears and delicate facial features. She lie curled in a ball on her side, facing him.

He reached out and brushed back her light red hair. It was a curly, snarled mess. A large bruise showed on one cheek. Her breathing was slow and even.

"Female?"

She didn't stir at all. He carefully pulled the blanket off her upper body. He saw more bruising on her pale arms and growled softly. Someone had beaten her. Her delicate-looking wrists had damaged skin from restraints. The cuts were inflamed, red and infected. The dress she wore had rips in the front at the top, exposing one rounded breast, but it was covered by material, a thin white cup.

He shifted his position, braced his knee against the floor, and carefully rolled her onto her back. It was easy to slide his arms under her and lift, blanket and all. She didn't weigh much and wasn't a big female.

He carried her out of the cell, her body limp in his arms.

Dovis approached him, looking furious. "That's a human."

"I know. Start opening the cells, except for the green alien. We'll toss in the guard's bracelet after the others flee. It should take him a minute or two to figure it out. Hopefully." He lowered his voice. "They can fight their way out together and give us cover. Everyone up in the bar should be too busy with them to notice us."

"We can't go without her." Dovis stared at the female's face. "My Mari would want us to save another of her kind."

"I wasn't planning on leaving her. I wouldn't be carrying her otherwise."

Dovis gave him a brief nod and took the bracelet.

"Signal the others to get to the shuttle and fire up the engines. It might be a good idea to leave the surface immediately while they hunt for their escaped prisoners."

Dovis nodded. "Can I shift?"

Cavas shook his head. "A Tryleskian traveling with one of your race is too memorable. We don't want anyone to suspect what ship we're on."

Chapter Two

Jill woke to bright lights and the terrifying sight of a human-like robot standing over her. Her mouth opened, a scream ready to tear from her throat.

"It's a medical android. He's repairing your injuries and wiping out the last traces of infection from your cuts. Just hold still," a deep voice stated.

She twisted her head and saw a tall, large male. He wasn't human— but his race wasn't unknown to her. She'd met an alien like him before. "Did the other one send you?"

He stepped closer. "Other one?"

"He was like you, only he had black hair. You look similar in the face."

"What was his name?"

"He never said."

He came even closer. "Tell me about him."

"Where am I?" She glanced around again, leery of the robot, but he wasn't hurting her.

"You're safe on *The Vorge*. My name is Cavas. We found you unconscious inside a holding cell under a bar on the planet Flax. No one here is going to hurt you. Please tell me about the male. I believe it may have been my younger brother."

She felt a tinge of sympathy for him. She didn't have any family left alive, though she wished it. "Earth sold me. They claimed they'd passed a law that made being jobless illegal. I was put on a transport, kept in a cage, and ended up being sold to some rich alien who already had other slaves."

"Human slaves?"

She shook her head. "They were various alien females. The man who bought me was on a business trip when I arrived at his house. The head slave, Cia, got me implanted with a translator, gave me a rundown on what was expected of me, and warned me to do everything I was told if I wanted to live. I was kept on a twenty-foot leash with a collar around my neck to make sure I couldn't run away. I was there for a few weeks before he came back." Revulsion made her shudder. "You should have seen him. He wasn't anything like *you*."

Cavas gave her a questioning look.

"You're mostly human-looking. Two arms. Two legs. This alien...wasn't. He resembled a big bug, with four legs and six arms." She shuddered. I was told lots of horror stories about what would happen to me if I acted up or refused to take orders from our master. I didn't want to end up in a sex house being raped by dozens of aliens every day. Cia, the slave in charge of me, said it was the second worst place a slave could end up. She also said because I was human, they might rent out my womb to birth alien babies. I believed her. At least, enough to think submitting to one alien sounded better than many. She assured me our owner didn't want young. That was a bonus in my mind. Why bring a new life into that hell, right?"

He nodded. "That would be tragic. But what about my brother?"

"I'm getting to that. The alien who bought me returned from his trip. Then I saw him—and I just couldn't let him touch me. He undressed and ordered me to lie on the bed." She shook her head. "I've always hated bugs. The thought of allowing him to crawl on top of me was too much. I flipped out and tried to run away from him. That pissed him off. He grabbed my chain and started pulling me toward him, yelling about how he'd make it extra painful for me. So, I fought harder."

The robot backed away and went to the wall, where it seemed to shut down.

Cavas held out his hand to her. "It's done. You've been treated for all your injuries. Did the alien who bought you cause your injuries?"

She hesitated only briefly before deciding to trust him. He'd gotten her medical help, after all.

Of course, it might be a trap...but the other alien who'd looked like him had tried to save her. She was willing to give him the benefit of the doubt.

Jill let him help her sit up. His big hands were gentle. He released her as soon as she swung her legs over the edge of the bed.

She took stock of her body. Her clothes were torn and dirty, but her bruises were nearly faded. The cuts were sealed. Her skin wasn't red anymore where the cuffs had broken her skin. "No," she finally continued. "That happened later. While I was fighting bug alien, he fell and impaled his head on some stupid piece of sharp sculpture in his bedroom. This horrible screeching sound came from him, and four guards rushed into the bedroom. Two of them tried to help him, and the other two grabbed me."

Cavas cocked his head, listening patiently.

She openly studied his eyes. They were pretty, for a cat guy. He was also huge. "When the guards tried to pull the alien bug free from the sharp sculpture...his head came off." She watched Cavas closely, unsure how he'd react when she admitted to accidently killing the jerk who'd bought her.

"Good. That means there's one less slave buyer."

His response surprised her. "You're not mad?"

"No."

"What do you plan on doing with me?"

"I'll get you food, give you access to a shower and clean clothing. You're safe here. No one is going to sell or harm you. Please answer my questions first, though. My brother is missing. What do you know?"

She hoped he was telling the truth. "After the bug alien died, his guards were pretty mad. They were supposed to turn me over to the authorities for execution. One of them said they should claim his death was an accident, and sell me instead to earn money, since they were out of a job. The other guards agreed. They took me to this super nice house. I heard one of them say something about it belonging to the alien who owns the planet."

"Yorlian Trevis."

By his snarled tone, she could guess Cavas didn't like whoever that was. "No one said that name. They asked to speak to the 'overlord.' The overlord wasn't there, but the big red-skinned alien who answered the door bought me. I was taken into a basement and locked inside a large cage. *That's* when I saw the one who looks like you. I mean, same race.

28

His hair was black and his eyes were blue. He was already locked up down there."

"He didn't tell you his name?"

She shook her head. "We weren't allowed to talk to each other. There were other red-skinned guards watching us. When the guards weren't paying attention, the one who looked like you would use his hands, trying to signal to me. He wanted the metal decorations in my hair to pick the lock on his cage. I removed them and tossed them to him when it was safe. It worked. He got his door open, beat down both guards, and then let me out of my cage. It happened super fast. He said he was going to help me escape."

"Crath wouldn't have abandoned a slave. We're protective of females. Did you happen to see any scars on him?"

She gave a nod. "He had one on his neck." She reached up and pointed at her own to show where it was located.

That seemed to excite the lion guy. "That's my brother. What happened next?"

"We ran. He told me that he had a shuttle hidden to get us off the planet, and he'd take me somewhere safe. He also said my timing was perfect, since they were just about to move him to a more secure location. Only...we didn't make it. A group of aliens caught us. We both fought, but they shot him with some kind of knockout darts. Me too. Next thing I knew, I woke up in another cell. There were two green aliens that looked like toads in the cell with me. They wanted to know if I was 'the Tressie's life-lock.'"

"Tryleskian."

"Sorry. I'm new with alien names. That sounds right. I told them I didn't know. Then they asked me where he was taking me. I lied, saying I wasn't sure. I had hoped that he'd escape a second time and maybe he'd come back to take me to his shuttle. He was my only hope."

"I'm sure Crath would have come back for you if he were able. *Are you his life-lock?*"

"I still don't know what that means."

"His mate?"

Jill was stunned. "No! I mean, we said like twenty words max to each other. If even that. We were running for our lives." A memory surfaced. "He mentioned his brother!" She stared up at him. "You?"

"What did he say?"

"'My brother will help you stay safe.' I think those were his exact words."

The tall male sighed. "That makes sense. Crath must have meant our older brother. Cathian and some males on his crew have life-locked to human females, including our cousin. You'd call it marriage. We've joked that *The Vorge* has become a human sanctuary for females. Do you know where they took my brother?"

She tried to think, focusing on being locked in that tiny room where she was questioned. Something else clicked. "They said I might see him again if he won me in a fight. They laughed, saying that was the most likely outcome since the overlord would find weaker males to go against him to make sure he stayed alive. I was pretty beat up and not feeling well. Then the toad aliens took me to another place. It was a dark cell, and

30

I was shivering from the cold. One gave me a blanket. I passed out, sure I was going to die. And then...I woke here."

Cavas stepped forward and offered his hand once more. "Let's get you cleaned and fed. Did you ever hear of something called the pits?"

She'd taken his hand to ease herself off the tall med bed, but froze at his question, staring directly into his eyes. Jill nodded warily.

He leaned in, getting close. He *did* have beautiful eyes. The shape and golden color reminded her of the eyes of a lion. She didn't fear him...but she *did* fear the memory of Cia's stories.

"What do you know about the pits? It's important."

"Cia said our master was a regular at the pits, which is also called the arena. That was another reason never to make him angry. It's somewhere deep in the desert, where arrested criminals are sent if they're sentenced to die. The prisoners are forced to fight each other to the death to entertain the rich. They bet large sums of money on the outcomes. Cia insisted all the men who go bring one or two of their sex slaves to the fights. It's like a status thing, to show us off to their friends...but she warned that sometimes, it's also how owners get rid of slaves they grow tired of or angry with. Owners bet on a fighter and offer their slaves as rewards, extra incentives to the criminals if their wagers win." Jill shuddered. "She also told me what happens then. If it's true, it's a nightmare."

He helped her off the table to stand. "What?"

She gazed up at him, craning her neck because he was almost a foot taller, and he stood so close. "The slaves are thrown into the arena from the stands. Only one person ever walks out of the arena alive. That's the rule. The women are raped and then murdered by the criminals who win the fights. If they make it extra entertaining for the audience, by prolonging the abuse, they're offered more incentives...extra food, time off to heal before their next fight."

He snarled.

She snatched her hand of out his. The sound he'd made was terrifying.

Cavas backed away. "My anger isn't directed at you. Apologies. The idea that Crath might have been taken to fight for his life...that's what upsets me. You're in no danger. I give my vow."

"You believe they took him to the pits?"

"It fits. Tryleskians mostly run that planet. To have one fight would draw spectators. My brother is an excellent fighter. The criminal who took him might want to make some money off Crath."

She nodded hesitantly. "I'd really like that shower and clean clothing now. You said there are other humans here? Could I meet them?"

He nodded. "Of course. Follow me."

Cavas tried to get a handle on his boiling rage. Had Beltsen Vellar known how sick and twisted his old friend Trevis had become? What had his father been thinking by putting Crath's life into a criminal's hands?

He opened the door to the guest cabin next to his and waved the female inside. "You never told me your name."

She entered, openly gazing around. "Jill. This is very nice."

"It's your new home for now."

She spun quickly. "I live alone? No one is going to bother me?"

"Yes, alone. This is your private cabin. No one on *The Vorge* will harm you in any way. As a matter of fact, all the male crew members, besides the Pods, are already life-locked to females. It means they would not have an interest in you."

"The Pods?"

"Small white aliens." He demonstrated their low height with a motion of his hand. "The Pods don't take mates or have sex with others. When they reproduce, they just decide to, and they have little Pods on their own. I should also warn you that they can read minds. It's not something they do to invade your privacy. It's just as natural to them as us seeing or hearing with our senses. They don't share what they learn with others, unless my brother has concerns. Cathian might ask them to scan your thoughts to make sure you're not a threat to his crew or this ship."

That stunned her. "Me? Is that a joke?" She wanted to snort. Then Jill remembered that she'd already told him she'd killed the alien who'd bought her. "The bug alien's death was self-defense. I can't say I'm sorry he's dead, but I didn't want to be raped."

His expression softened. "I'm *glad* the slave owner is dead. No one here would think badly of you for that. Truly. If you're unsure whether I'm being honest, or believe this is a trick to falsely earn your trust, maybe thinking of doing something rash or trying to escape...there's no need for that. This ship is a human sanctuary. All the females willingly agreed to life-lock with the males they're with. They have deep feelings for each other. Tryleskians with honor do not believe in slavery or rape. We abhor it. Cathian is the ambassador who represents the residents from our home world. He's also my brother. We have honor, Jill."

She stared at him with trepidation. It reminded him of how fragile her race must feel around aliens that were bigger and stronger. Humans didn't have sharp teeth, claws, or even the muscle mass to defend themselves against most alien kind.

"You've been through a lot, from what you've shared with me, including your own planet Earth betraying you." He reached up and touched his chest. "I give my solemn vow that everything I say to you is true. *The Vorge* is a sanctuary. On your planet, does that word translate into a safe place to live, where no harm befalls you?"

"Yes."

"No male will force anything on you. You are not a slave anymore. This is your home."

She opened her mouth, then closed it.

"My cousin's life-lock, Lilly, has family on Earth. It's not safe for her to visit but my brother said she communicates with them every few weeks using the bridge to call home. We know your planet hasn't been honest with your people about selling females to other races, nor have they admitted to nearly causing wars by their actions in space. They've attacked a peaceful planet to steal from them. There have been more transgressions, but that is the most widely known. It wouldn't be safe to send you back. Those in power on Earth could kill you to prevent their lies from being exposed."

"That sounds about right." Her thin shoulders slumped. "I already figured out I can't ever go home. They'd just sell me again, especially after I've been labeled a criminal."

She looked too defenseless to ever be a threat. "You said not having a job is a crime there?"

"Apparently. That's what they said when they showed up at my place to arrest me, two hours after I quit my job."

"Why did you quit?"

"My boss was a creep. He wanted me to blow him. I flat-out refused, so he tried to force me. I had to punch him in the face to get away, and I immediately quit. I knew I couldn't ever go back."

"Blow?" He didn't know that term.

Her pale cheeks turned pink. It was oddly attractive. "All employers have access to our medical records. He must have looked mine up, because he knew I wasn't on an implant to prevent pregnancy. That meant he couldn't have sex with me. Instead, he decided my mouth would work just as well. It's called oral sex. Putting my mouth on his dick. Is that clear enough to understand what he wanted? He had grabbed my hair and tried to push me to my knees in front of him. I fought back and got away."

Anger boiled under Cavas's skin yet again. "Why wasn't he arrested? He should have been stripped of power, whipped, and locked away for such a crime."

The pink left her cheeks, and she studied him again before speaking. "It used to be like that. I mean, men got punished for sexually assaulting women, but then the birthrates drastically changed over several decades.

35

Women fought hard for equality ages ago, but it all went to hell real fast when there were way fewer boys than girls being born. You'd think women would rule then, but that wasn't the case. Men were given unfair advantages, including jobs that put them in charge and earning more money.

"Bottom line—men are rare. Women are plenty. To put a man in prison is seen as a bad thing, since men have sperm. They control who can have babies, with some women even paying huge amounts of money for the privilege. A man would have to kill a few people just to be considered dangerous enough to be arrested. Crimes like beating up a woman or even sexual assault are..."

She trailed off, shaking her head. "The police will just tell you to stay away from the man to avoid it happening again. Most women don't even bother to file charges. There's no point, since they won't do anything to the men. I had a friend who was raped a few years ago. Do you know what the cops said to her?"

Cavas tried to imagine a world like that. He couldn't. It sounded horrible for the females. "What?"

"That she should feel lucky—because he managed to get her pregnant during the attack. She didn't have to pay some guy a huge fee to birth a baby. She ended up having to give her daughter up for adoption to a rich woman, since she could barely support herself. How in the hell was that *lucky*? It broke her heart."

"That's tragic." He couldn't imagine having to give a child to someone else. "Would you like to communicate with your family on Earth? I'm sure the crew would be happy to do it."

36

The human turned, peering around the room. "I don't have anyone left...but thank you for the offer. You said something about a shower? Is it here? I've never been on a spaceship before. The cage in the cargo hold didn't really count."

He moved around her, leading her to the bathroom and showing her how to use everything. She kept her distance, seeming almost fearful. Cavas felt a bit sorry for her. After all she'd been through, he could understand her mistrust. He exited the bathroom but paused at the door.

"I'll send a female to you with clothing. Is it permissible if she enters your cabin while you get clean? That way, you'll have an Earth face and female to speak to when you're done."

She nodded.

"I'll leave now. She'll make sure you're fed, too."

He'd barely left her cabin before he'd touched the ship's communication device, activating it for the entire crew to hear. "I need one of the life-locks in our guest's quarters. The female needs clothing and food. Whoever comes can just enter while she's showering. Her name is Jill. I'm going to be on the bridge searching the planet's surface for the fighting arena."

Cathian answered immediately. "An arena?"

Cavas's fury returned. "It seems our youngest littermate might be fighting for his life to amuse those bastards. Yorlian Trevis hosts death matches somewhere in the desert for the entertainment of his wealthy residents."

His older brother snarled. "I'll meet you on the bridge. Nara will take the new female clothing. I'll have Midgel prepare her a favorite Earth dish and drop it off."

Cavas didn't need to hear more. The rescued female would be tended to. Crath needed to be found and rescued before he was murdered.

Then they could deal with their father.

Chapter Three

Jill finally felt clean, and whatever the robot had done to her was appreciated. All her injuries were healing at an accelerated rate. The bruises had already faded completely. She wrapped a towel around her body and hesitantly opened the door to peer into the large cabin.

The sight of two human women waiting about eight feet away was a relief. The lion man alien hadn't lied to her. She stepped out, studying them. She couldn't help but look for signs of abuse, but she found none. They weren't even wearing collars, or one of the wristbands that could cause pain—something else Cia had warned her about.

"I'm Nara," the blonde greeted. "This is Sara. Welcome to *The Vorge*. It's a big ambassador vessel from the planet Tryleskian. My husband— otherwise known as a life-lock—is Cathian, the captain and ambassador of this space love boat." She grinned.

The brunette with big green eyes smiled, as well. "We call it that now as a joke. Earth sold me, too. Cavas said they did the same to you. Our home world sucks." She held a folded pile of clothing in her arms. "These are for you. My mate York overbuys for me, so I donated my clothes until we can get you some of your own. Keep them if you want."

"I'm Jillian Yates. Call me Jill." She glanced between them. "Are we really safe here?"

Sara set the clothing down—then surprised her with a hug. "Yes."

Jill felt the rounded bump of her stomach, and she gasped, looking between them when Sara backed up. The woman touched her slightly extended belly and grinned. "I'm carrying a blue baby in there. At least I *hope* this kid looks like York. He's a Parri. Think big and blue."

Sara was pregnant with an alien! Jill had heard it was possible, been warned her womb might be rented out, but to actually know it was true came as a shock. "You're happy about it?"

"Yep! We tried hard to get pregnant." Sara winked. "I love York. I take it you haven't been in space long?"

Jill shook her head. "About a month. I think. Time is hard to keep track of."

Nara came closer. "I read your medical scans. I hope that doesn't offend you. I wanted to know what we were dealing with. I'm kind of in charge of the humans onboard. We don't have a counselor for therapy, but we're here if you want to talk to someone about whatever horrors you were exposed to. The scans done on you showed no signs of sexual abuse, but you were beaten. Is that correct?" she asked gently.

Jill nodded. She just hoped they didn't ask for details. She shared enough with Cavas. She didn't want to go over them again, or even *think* about the alien bug jerk who'd died. It still made her shudder.

Sara looked relieved. "We're glad the scans were right. I mean, a beating is bad enough, but it could have been much worse. I was lucky enough to be rescued before the sicko alien who bought me was able to pick me up. He owned a harem of sex slaves. I had to stay in a shelter for a bit with other alien women who'd been forced into slavery. Let's just say that people from Earth aren't well-liked by aliens. That's how I met York. He was nice to me, and not prejudiced like so many others."

"I met Cathian after getting arrested for smuggling medicine for sick people. It was bullshit. They gave me a choice of going to prison, where I'd have become food for the inmates, or becoming a sex slave for a year. This crew bought my contract for their captain, and...we fell in love!"

Nara chuckled. "The point is, nothing you've been through will shock us. The other two humans on this ship are Mari and Lilly. Mari's parents sold her into slavery as a kid, which was just shitty. Luckily, the aliens who bought her put her to work as a mechanic. She wasn't severely abused but they did a number on her head. She had the whole slave mentality down pat. Then she was freed and got a job on our ship, and Dovis fell in love with her. Lilly was kidnapped off a ship while working on a research vessel and sold to a whorehouse. She broke free before her first customer could hurt her and ran straight into Raff, and they're together now. He's my husband's cousin."

Sara nodded. "Dovis is like an alien werewolf shifter. Don't freak out when you see him. He looks scary but he won't hurt you. Also, don't flip out if you see a stranger who almost looks human, but not quite. That's Dovis when he's *not* in werewolf form. But since he and Mari got together, he sticks to being in skin more."

Jill glanced between them, her mind spinning. "Okay."

"We're dumping too much information on you, aren't we? Sorry." Nara motioned to the table. "Are you hungry? We brought you clothing and food."

"Let me put something on." Jill moved around them to grab a shirt and pants from the pile before rushing back into the bathroom, where she dressed fast. The clothing was a little baggy but it was clean. She took a

41

few deep breaths before returning to the women again. They were nice, if not a little overwhelming, and so far, she liked them.

She felt a little self-conscious taking a seat at the table, but hunger drove her to dig into the food. It was a blue rice with purple veggies, and cooked meat that tasted like beef. It was pretty good. The women hesitated before sitting at the table, too. Sara poured her a drink of water from a pitcher on the table.

"Thank you. Sorry if I'm being rude. I can't remember the last time I ate."

"Don't worry about it. Do you have any questions?"

Jill looked up and held Nara's gaze. "So many. I just don't want to be ungrateful."

"You won't be. That's why we're here. Ask away."

"Are we *really* safe on this ship? Are you really...um...free?"

Nara didn't look offended. "I'll be honest with you. There are tons of shitty aliens out in space, and a lot of them think women are only good for being sex slaves. It's not like that with any of the people on this ship. We're not going to spring any nasty surprises on you. We're like a family. You may be considering going back to Earth or finding somewhere else to live, but it might not be safe. At least our guys protect us."

Sara agreed. "Most aliens would try to kidnap you for sexual slavery. Some just hate us for being human. Earth doesn't have the best reputation with some of them. Without going into detail, let's just say some Earth ships have done some bad shit. The people on this vessel, even though they're aliens, are some of the best you'll ever meet."

Jill wanted so badly to believe them. "Cavas said it's a sanctuary for humans."

Nara chuckled. "That's a good description. He nailed it."

"What's the price, though?" Jill glanced between them. "To eat your food, for this room, the clothes? Nothing in life is free. What are they going to expect in return?"

Sara reached over and gently patted her arm. "We help out where we can. That's it. Nothing nefarious going on here. I just kind of sit around talking to people who are on duty, now that I'm pregnant. No one wants me to lift anything or stay on my feet for long."

"I've been trailing Mari and helping her keep parts of the ship working." Nara shrugged. "The guys don't really expect much from us, to be honest. We're not as strong or big as them. Just don't offer to help Midgel in the kitchen. She's our cook, and she's territorial as hell."

Sara chuckled. "She looks as if her mom might have been a mouse and her father a short human. Don't be shocked—or mention it. She also gets upset if you ask her about ever getting married. She's kind of anti-man, and has sworn to stay single forever."

"In her culture, women are used as breeders. She's had to do that a few times," Nara added. "I don't think it was a great experience, and she never wants to do it again. That's why she works on this ship. She's safe from her males forcing her to have their babies. Our guys would kill anyone who tried to snatch her. She's protected here."

Jill glanced between them again, skeptical. "You're saying I can live on this ship, and no one is going to make me have sex with them, or something equally bad? I just want to know what to expect."

Nara's expression softened. "Every man on this ship who's interested in sex has a wife, except for Cavas. Our alien guys don't cheat. You're *safe*. No one is going to touch you or do bad things to you. Just help around the ship, treat everyone like you'd wish to be treated, and that's it. We have the room, and you're safer here than if we dropped you off on a planet somewhere. Humans become targets on their own. Some slaver would grab and sell you. Or worse, they'd just steal you for themselves. Either option wouldn't be good, if you want to avoid being sexually abused. *The Vorge* is the sanctuary Cavas told you it was."

"It'll be nice to have another human aboard." Sara leaned closer, holding her gaze. "We're not lying, Jill. I totally know what it's like to get screwed over and dropped into a bad situation. Our world leaders did that by selling me to aliens. We're totally on the level. Just help out where you can around the ship and that's all that will ever be asked of you. I swear. We all work as a team."

"We're just like a family." Nara looked and sounded completely sincere. "A tight one. We all care about each other."

Jill finally relaxed slightly, blinking back grateful tears. "What about Cavas? Do I have to worry about him? You said he's not married."

"He's an honorable Tryleskian," Nara explained. "They don't believe in forcing women into anything. Most of their race are good guys. They'd kill a male for hurting a woman in any way. Rape is a death offense on their planet. Of course, there's always some bad mixed in with the good. Cavas isn't normally a part of our crew. Do you want to know why he's here?"

Jill nodded.

44

"Cathian, Cavas, and Crath are triplets, but not identical. Tryleskians have multiple babies at once. Their father, Beltsen, is a major asshole. He's *not* honorable."

"Understatement. He's a rich, powerful politician type. Earth style." Sara made a dirty face. "You know what I'm saying. You can't trust him as far as you can throw him. He's as corrupt as they come."

"We have some blackmail material to keep Beltsen Vellar from trying to take this ship from us." Nara hesitated. "Let's just say we don't follow the orders he gives because he's a total douchebag. Cathian is their world's ambassador. This ship goes with the job. *The Vorge* is our home. We're not losing it just because we won't break laws when he orders us to. Anyway…Beltsen asked Cavas to come after us to get the evidence we have. When he refused, their asshole father had Crath kidnapped, and he's being held on the planet you were just rescued from. Beltsen is basically holding his own son's life over this crew to get that evidence."

Sara cradled her rounded belly. "We have zero expectations that Beltsen won't kill one of his own sons to get what he wants. We need to find Crath. Cathian has already reached out to all the other siblings to let them know what's going on and warned them not to trust their father, so more of them aren't used against us."

Nara nodded. "They're pissed at their father. It insults them all that he'd do something this shitty. It's dishonorable, and even shocking. You're supposed to love your kids. Not have one kidnapped to try to force your other son into doing bad shit. The siblings know we're searching for Crath to save him. That's how you were found. Cavas and Dovis were searching for Crath in those cells, but found you instead. They weren't going to leave you down there. You're a human who needed help. It's what we do."

The alien man with blue eyes who'd helped her escape flashed through Jill's mind. "I think I saw him. The brother."

Nara met her gaze. "Cavas told us. Both of you were recaptured before Crath could get you to his shuttle. He would have brought you to us if you'd managed to get off the planet. We'll find him, though, and when we do, then we'll deal with Beltsen Vellar. Otherwise known as worst father ever and a major asshole. This shit has got to stop. He keeps screwing with us. This time he's gone too far."

Sara leaned in, adding, "The other siblings are working on removing him from power on their planet. We have to find Crath, though, before they can really go after him. Beltsen will order Crath killed in retaliation for sure. Once Beltsen is kicked off his throne, as they say, one of the brothers in the next litter will take his seat. We'll no longer be given orders, and we won't have to worry about losing our home." She tapped the table with her finger. "This ship."

"Litter?" Jill frowned. "Is that what you said?"

"Tryleskians have litters. Multiple births with each pregnancy." Sara patted her stomach. "I'm glad I'm having a Parri. Multiples are rare for them."

"A typical litter is between three to five babies. I've been assured by Cathian that they're smaller than human infants at birth. Like two pounds each. The upside to that is, Tryleskian males only go into heat every three years. That's the only time they can knock up their wives. It's not like women will be endlessly pregnant, marrying one of their men."

46

Jill tried to wrap her head around what Nara just said. "Wow."

"Tryleskians can totally have sex when they aren't in heat, of course." Nara chuckled. "That was one of the first questions I had when I learned about their heats. Was I locking myself to a guy who would only do me every three years? Wait until you see Cathian." She winked. "It would have been torture if that were the case."

"He looks a lot like Cavas," Sara explained.

Nara jerked slightly, then reached down, lifting a round disk. She pressed it. "What's up?"

"Mandatory meeting in the dining hall," a gruff male voice stated.

"We'll be right there. I'm with Sara and Jill. Thanks, Dovis." She pushed the button and stood.

Sara did too.

Jill hesitated, unsure what to do.

Nara motioned to her. "Come on. You're part of the crew now."

"Okay." Jill got up from her seat. "What about shoes?"

"You're fine. We'll replicate some for you later." Sara closed her eyes and got a weird look on her face...like she was concentrating really hard.

Jill glanced at Nara. "What is she doing? Is she okay?"

"She does that when she's thinking at the Pods."

"The aliens who can read minds?"

"Yes. Brace yourself when you see them. They look like eggs with thin arms and legs. The Pods are super nice, though. You don't have to be afraid of anyone on this ship. I promise. We really are like a close family. I can't say it enough."

47

Sara opened her eyes and moved toward the door. "I asked them to make her shoes and reminded them she was scanned in medical, so they can get the sizing right." She glanced at Jill. "It'll be after the meeting, since we're all needed now. Sorry."

Jill followed behind them as they left her cabin and headed toward the dining hall. She felt a lot better after talking to the women. Cavas had seemed nice enough, but he was an alien. Her trust in them wasn't the best after all she'd been through. But now she knew he'd been telling her the truth. She was safe on the ship, with aliens who wouldn't hurt her.

* * * * *

Cavas took a sip of his fruity drink and scanned the data that had been uploaded to his handheld device from one of the drones they'd sent down to the planet. He looked up, scowling at Cathian. "Are you sure you need to keep your entire crew apprised of our plan?"

His brother nodded. "We're going to need their help, and we don't keep secrets from each other. This isn't the military, Cavas."

He inwardly winced. It was another reminder that his life had been drastically altered. He didn't feel regret, so much as a sense of shock. It had never crossed his mind to resign from his duties. He'd been in line to command their entire military within a few years. That had been his ambition for as long as he could remember.

Now that future was gone.

Cathian seemed to read his thoughts. As brothers born in the same litter, they had a strong bond and knew each other well. "Are you certain you don't want to replace our father when he's forced from his position?

It would give you great power, and you'd be in control of our entire family's empire. You're second born of the first litter our parents birthed. It's your right, since I sure as hell don't want to live full time on our planet."

"No. Let the litter born after ours take that duty. I'd rather stay here." He studied Cathian's face. "If you'll have me."

"You always have a place by my side."

That was a worry off his shoulders. "Crath sure as hell won't want to take over father's position, either."

Cathian snorted. "No. He would consider it a punishment. All three of us have been great disappointments to our father."

"You and Crath, perhaps. You refused to step down as an ambassador when he wanted you to. It was supposed to be a temporary position for you to learn how to play nice with aliens. Father planned to personally groom you to take his place in the next few decades at home. And Crath has always had wanderlust. Once he learned how to fly a shuttle, there was no keeping him at home. I was the only one in our litter to follow the path our father wanted. He looked forward to me leading our military."

Cathian grinned at Cavas, knowing he was being teased. "Not anymore. You resigned. You're a disappointment to him now, too."

"I don't feel bad about that. He's not who I believed him to be."

"No shit." Cathian growled, his humor gone. "I want to kill him with my bare hands."

49

"As first born, it's your right. He's brought shame to our entire family with his actions. Let's get Crath back first."

"Agreed."

The doors to the dining hall opened, and Cathian's crew began to enter. Cavas studied them. York, Dovis, and Raff were fierce fighters. The rest of them though were weak links. None of them would cut it in the military except for the Pods. They were an asset with their mental abilities.

All three of the small aliens glanced at him with smiles, reading his mind.

He gave them a nod and placed his data pad on the table.

Everyone else arrived, including the thin cook. She sat far from the others. He'd be leery of trusting her, with the standoffish way she acted, but the Pods would know if Midgel were a spy.

Cathian stood, giving his life-lock Nara a kiss before moving to the center of the room. He motioned for everyone to sit.

Cavas couldn't help but throw a few curious glances at Jill. He hadn't expected her to attend. She sat between Sara and Nara, keeping her chin down.

He shot a glance at One, thinking at the Pod. *Is the new human a threat?*

One mouthed *no*.

That was enough for Cavas. He trusted the Pods. He knew their history and the absolute loyalty they felt toward his oldest brother. Cathian had rescued them from criminals and kept them safe. Mind-

50

reading aliens were in high demand on the black market. Their lives would have remained hellish if they hadn't found safe harbor on the ship.

"We have found the arena. It's a few hundred miles from the colony, situated very close to a mountain. Scans from the drones we sent down have shown a large cavern in the side of that mountain. It's probably where their prisoners are being held." Cathian tapped his data pad and flattened it in his hand. An image appeared on the wall next to him. It was a vid the drone had taken of the large outdoor arena, and two massive doors in the side of the mountain, hundreds of feet off the ground. A thin walkway connected them to one of the platforms near the top of the arena. The doors to the mountain were open. "There are fifty-four life signs inside the mountain. One of them is hopefully Crath."

"We're hopeful that Crath isn't being forced to fight deadly opponents, since our father will want him alive. It's a secure place to hold him, though." Cavas stood, moving next to the image. "I plan to go down to see one of the fights and hopefully sneak inside that cavern, to search for our brother."

Red dots lit up. There were dozens of them. "These are the guards posted," Cathian informed the crew. "The drone tagged them because they wear uniforms. It won't be easy to get past them. We've scanned the side and back of the mountain. It appears there are no other alternative ways inside. That means entering the arena, reaching a high point where that bridge is located, and crossing it into the mountain cavern."

Cavas took over again. This was the difficult part of the plan that he hated most. "I'll play the role of a wealthy slave owner going to see the fights this evening." He glanced at Jill, but she kept her chin down. "We had our drones scanning life signs on all the shuttles coming from and going to the arena. There have been three fights since we got them in place. There are mass transports to bring spectators, but those people are most likely seated well below the walkway. We're certain those higher platforms are viewing options for the wealthy. They're closest to the walkway. Life scans confirm the wealthy assholes in private transports travel with females. Probably a sex slave. Jill, is that correct? Your source of information said it was a status thing among the wealthy males, bringing a female?"

Jill looked up, met his gaze, and gave a slight nod.

"Every private shuttle has had at least one female, sometimes two," Cathian grunted. "That's the bad news."

"I hate this...but we need one of you females to play the part of a sex slave," Cavas said quietly. "It will put one of you in danger," he admitted. "We thought about flying a shuttle over the walkway to gain access, but there are too many guards, and we must worry about whether the caverns are rigged to blow. I've seen that before on a few missions to retrieve captured prisoners from pirates. Rather than risk them being rescued; the pirates detonated their holding cells."

"I wish Marrow were here," Cathian said. "She'd be perfect for this. Unfortunately, she is not." He shot an angry look at Cavas.

"I needed her to fly my shuttle and pretend to be me. Father would either move Crath or have him killed if he suspected I was attempting a rescue. I know Marrow is tough and a good fighter, but she's also a hell of a pilot. I won't put it past our father to try to have me captured—and

Marrow won't be caught." He glanced at York. "No offense to your flying skills, but Marrow's the best pilot on *The Vorge*."

"I wouldn't have left my Sara, anyway," York answered. "She's pregnant. And no, you can't take her down there."

"Of course not." Cavas wouldn't ask that.

"I'll do it." Nara stood.

"No," Cathian snarled.

She met his gaze with a glare. "Are you kidding me right now? I'm in charge of the humans, and I say it's me."

"*Not* you."

Nara held his brother's gaze without even flinching at his harsh tone. "Let's be honest. Midgel would freak." She glanced at the cook. "No offense. It would be hell for you to be led around by a collar." She motioned to the female with long hair on Dovis's lap. "Mari is the most docile of us humans, but she's not a fighter. It would be her and Cavas alone down there. She'd be horrible backup." This time, she glanced at Mari. "No offense. And Lilly could put up a decent fight if they got into trouble, but she's been throwing up. Therefore, it's *me*."

Raff growled, staring at his female. "You're sick?"

She shrugged. "My stomach has been upset a few times. It's no big deal. I can do it." She stared at Cathian. "I owe you guys my life. I'm in if you need me."

"No!" Raff snarled. "I'm taking you to see the android."

"Nara is right about one thing," Mari suddenly said. "I was raised as a slave. I'm the best one of us to pull this off. You should take me, Cavas."

Dovis snarled. "You are submissive. What if there's a battle?"

All the couples began to argue loudly, while Midgel got up and fled the room.

Cavas simply watched them, feeling a headache coming on. It was nice that most of the females were willing to risk their lives to attempt a rescue of his littermate. Too bad their males were all having a fit.

Chapter Four

Jill sat quietly, watching the crew. Some of the women were yelling at their husbands, arguing why they should be the one to go. Then she glanced at Cavas. He stood there with his eyes closed, a pained expression on his handsome alien face. It was clear he wasn't happy to ask one of the women to volunteer to put themselves in danger.

She looked around again, studying the alien men facing off against their wives. All of them appeared worried, upset, fearful—and that's when it sank in.

They must honestly love those women.

She bit her lip...then found herself standing. She put two fingers in her mouth and gave a shrill whistle.

Everyone went quiet, gawking at her.

She pulled her fingers from her mouth and turned to Nara. "I'll do it."

Nara shook her head. "No."

"I'm not married, certainly not pregnant or sick, and you said I should help out on this ship when it's needed. Technically it's not *on* the ship, but it's the same, right?" She glanced around at everyone else. "You guys saved my life. I owe you. I just spent almost a month wearing a collar on that damn planet. I was trained on how to act by another slave. I don't have any skills for use on a spaceship, but I'm good at keeping my shit together under pressure. I also won't hesitate to fight to protect myself. I've survived this long by doing so. Let me do it."

Nara stepped closer. "You just got free, Jill. You're emotionally in a bad place right now. None of us would be."

"I'm a little screwed up in the head after all I've been through. I'm not denying that. You also made it clear we need to rescue Crath in order to keep this ship and crew safe. I was listening, Nara. It's important that we find him, and I owe him for getting me out of that cage. He tried to take me to his shuttle. I *want* to go after him. It's only right."

Jill turned to Cavas. His eyes were open, and he was staring at her with a scowl. "I don't have great fighting skills, but I'm not helpless. I can take orders, keep my mouth shut, and I was instructed on how to act if I was ever escorted to that arena. I'm your best bet."

Cavas hesitated. "We don't know you."

"What he means," one of the white little aliens stated, "is that he's not sure if you'll be motivated enough to do what is necessary to get Crath out of there. You could try to flee out of distrust of us, since you're new." The Pod studied her, going silent. Then he turned to Cavas. "She understands what's at stake, and trusts what Nara and Sara have said to her. She feels her best chance at survival is to stay with us. You can trust her. She's sufficiently motivated."

Jill felt slightly violated since her mind had just been read, but she understood. She stared at the white alien, thinking questions at it, curious to know if it would hear her.

"My name is One," it stated. "We were sold by our own people to criminals who used our mind-reading abilities to harm others. We not only read thoughts, but we feel pain if someone is being tortured if we're linked to them at the time. Our captors did that often. It was hellish, a term you understand. This crew saved us and now they keep us safe from being used in that way again. None of them would harm us or you. You can trust them."

The pod next to him spoke. "I'm Three. If you are captured, this crew will come for Cavas and you. They would risk their lives for yours. Each one of them thinks of you as a part of this crew now. Your life is valued."

Jill took a deep breath and blew it out, turning back to Cavas. "I'm the one you need to take with you. If a woman must go down there and put her butt on the line, it should be me. I owe you guys, and I'm not married. I owe your brother. And I'm all about paying my debts."

"She means that," one of the Pods stated.

"We didn't rescue you to put you back in danger," Dovis growled.

He did appear scary, even in skin. She tried to image him looking like a werewolf but failed. "I appreciate that, but let's be real. None of you really know me." She returned her attention to Cavas. "You saved me once. I trust you to get me out of there again if shit hits the fan. But if you have to send one of us women into danger, and the worst happens, losing *me* will hurt the least."

He didn't look pleased at that, but he nodded. "It's the logical choice."

There were some loud protests.

Cavas snarled louder. "Enough. Jill has volunteered. I've accepted." He shot a look at his brother. "None of your crew want their females in danger. This is the best solution. I'm without a life-lock. Jill is without one, too. Our losses will be the easiest on everyone if we fail."

"*No* loss is acceptable," Cathian stated emotionally.

"Agreed." Cavas hesitated before looking at Nara. "Can you help her find something suitable to wear and replicate the collar she once wore? I'll dress to fit the part. The drones have taken images of the wealthy slavers getting off those private shuttles. We'll meet in half an hour in front of the cargo bay. Since some of them have recently arrived, a fight must be taking place soon. We need to get down there as quickly as possible." He turned to Cathian. "I'll do my best to bring our littermate and Jill back safely."

Jill walked quickly toward the door, assuming Nara would follow. She just wanted out of that room and away from all those emotions. Including her own. She'd lost her mind to volunteer, but it did make the most sense. She owed these people her life. They could have left her in that cell. She'd have died there, or faced a horrible future at the hands of another slave owner if she'd recovered from her injuries.

"Wait up. Where are you going?"

She turned to force a smile for Nara. "Sorry."

"You don't have to do this."

"I do."

"You literally just got free today! No one would expect you to go back down there like this. It was brave and gutsy. Hell, *I'm* impressed, but I should be the one to go. I'm responsible for the humans on this ship."

"I'm doing this, Nara."

Nara stepped closer, peering deeply into her eyes. "But you're scared."

"I'd be an idiot if I weren't."

That caused the woman to smile. "True." Then she sobered. "Are you sure about this?"

"No, but I'm still going to do it."

Nara studied her silently.

"Do you want to know what I saw in that room?"

Her question seemed to surprise Nara. "What?"

"Guys who actually love their women. They weren't grabbing hold of you and being abusive when you were arguing. I saw real fear in their eyes. You have something here that I never thought I'd see in my lifetime."

"What's that?"

"Real love between couples. Five years ago, there was an outbreak of a coughing disease. We didn't have the money for treatments. My mom, three of her sisters, and my two female cousins got sick. They were all the blood family I had. My aunt was married, and so was one of her daughters. And the government was passing out antibiotic shots for free—to *men*. My uncle and my cousin's husband, like me, were spared catching the cough. I would have given my shots up in a heartbeat to save their lives, if I'd had any. But those bastards? They hid their shots just in case they needed them. They watched them die, doing nothing, until it was too late. I lost my entire family because those assholes were too fucking selfish to share drugs they didn't even need."

Nara appeared horrified. "I'm so sorry."

"Me too. It was a common story in the city that summer. Men weren't giving up their precious supply of antibiotics to save their wives, or even their own daughters. I wanted to kill my uncle, but men are protected on Earth."

"I remember it being that way," Nara admitted.

"The alien men on this ship honestly love their wives. The love you've found here, it's better than what's on Earth. I'm not going to let you lose that if I can help it. This ship is your home. As long as your husband manages to deal with his shitty dad and get his missing brother back, you get to keep this ship, right?"

"Yes," Nara sighed.

"Then I'm all in. You were willing to go down there. So am I. Is it terrifying? Yes. But now I have something to risk my life for—I want to be a part of this crew. I've got nothing left on Earth. Let me pull my weight."

Nara nodded. "Thank you."

Jill changed the subject. "The slaves down there don't wear much. Where do we go to get me a skimpy outfit?"

"We have a replicator. Cathian learned every known thing about Flax before they went down there, to find out how the locals dress. Let's go pull up the information, you can pick something you think will work, and then we'll have it made. It only takes a few minutes."

"Sounds good."

Jill pushed her fear back. The one thing the women in her family had taught her besides how to love was to always have the back of the people you care about most. She didn't know the crew, but they'd taken her in.

They were the only home she had left. She'd fight to keep it. The alternative wasn't an option.

* * * * *

Cavas hated the outfit he wore. The fact that Cathian stood smirking at him made it worse. "I look like a pompous, wealthy shaft-head."

His brother laughed. "You'll fit right in."

Cavas ran his hand down the open front slit of the lacy shirt, hating how much skin was exposed. The pants weren't much better. They reminded him more of fancy sleeping wear for the arrogant rich. The thick jeweled chains around his neck were irritating, along with the ones on each wrist.

Dovis approached, looking him up and down. He chuckled.

"Don't say a word," Cavas warned.

York approached next and whistled. "You look just like a successful slaver."

"Where is Jill? We need to leave." Cavas wanted to get to the surface of the planet and end the mission as quickly as possible.

"Right here."

He turned at the sound of her voice—and his eyes widened in shock.

Jill came around the corner of the corridor into the shuttle bay holding a long chain with a handle in her hands. The thin chain had about six feet of length and was attached to a collar around her delicate neck.

That wasn't what stunned him. Jill was breathtakingly beautiful. She also had a very appealing body. Most of it was on display. She was thin but had nice curves. Ones his fingers itched to stroke. The attraction he felt toward her made him angry. He'd saved her life. That made her off limits to his way of thinking. He shouldn't be having sexual thoughts about her.

"Where is the rest of your clothing? You wore more than that when I found you. Much more."

She paused, staring at him. "Remember when I said the guards decided to sell me to the planet owner? They made me wear my original outfit from Earth, thinking they'd get a better price if I seemed like I was fresh merchandise. This is more like what I wore while waiting for my first buyer to come home from his business trip. Cia and the other slaves dressed like this, too."

Cavas tried hard not to gawk, but it was difficult. The top she wore was little more than a tight strip of narrow material over her breasts. It hugged the bottom of her soft tempting breast mounds, but the tops of them were almost spilling out. And there was just a loose layer of thin material wrapped around her hips, attached by a useless string at the hip. It barely covered her sex in the front or her ass in the back.

"You're almost completely bared." He tried not to stare at her legs. They were small but shapely...and he could see so much of them. The only other thing she wore were little sandal-like shoes on her feet. Even those appeared delicate.

Humans were a fragile-looking race. He forced his gaze to her pale green eyes. They would haunt him if he wasn't able to keep her safe on their mission. He also noted that they were a beautiful color, reminding him of soft grass on his home world that grew on the cliffs by one of the Veller homes near the ocean.

She cocked her head. "Um, I'm pretending to be a *slave*." She walked up to him and held out the leash. "This is what they wear. I went with the non-sheer option. Some of the slaves in the house wore materials so thin that you could see everything. At least my important lady bits are covered in this." She glanced down at her chest. "Mostly. No nipples." She looked up at him. "Are we doing this or not?"

He ignored the leash handle. "I'll keep you safe." He turned, staring at his brother. "Be prepared for us to come back with possible enemy shuttles on our tail."

York cleared his throat. "We'll be ready to blow apart anything chasing you. Just make it back safe."

Dovis stepped close to Cavas. "Be careful. Don't punch them like you're a child."

He laughed. "I won't." He glanced back at Jill. "He was joking. I can fight. I'll do my best to protect you."

She gave a nod. "I'm not totally defenseless. Just so you know. Don't think I won't use this chain to hurt someone if the need arises."

She looked completely harmless, but he wasn't about to insult her. He respected her bravery to volunteer to go with him. He faced Cathian again. "Be safe. It's possible Yorlian Trevis has assigned space patrols since we let those prisoners go free. *The Vorge* could come under attack if they check behind the dead moon."

"We've deployed sensors on the other side. Anything flying this way won't be able to sneak up on us," York assured him. "This isn't our first time doing covert operations."

Cavas arched his eyebrows, looking at his brother.

Cathian grimly nodded. "It's sometimes my job to check out our alliances to make certain they're trustworthy. We're also well-armed to defend ourselves."

Cavas wasn't surprised his older littermate wouldn't blindly trust other aliens, and he was already aware of the extensive battlements on *The Vorge*. Not only was it the ambassador flagship for their planet, it was also capable of extreme defense in case of war. Tryleskians prided themselves on their fighting skills. To have a flagship that could easily be overtaken would have been an embarrassment. "We'll hopefully be back soon with Crath. Then we'll deal with our father and uncle."

"Uncle?" Jill asked.

"My biological father," Raff growled. "He needs to be killed, too."

"Let's go." Cavas didn't want to participate if an argument broke out between his cousin and his brother, about the ultimate fate of their fathers. It didn't matter to him if Beltsen was killed or just shamed into banishment. Either way, he'd be stripped of power. He walked through the cargo bay and headed up the ramp of the shuttle. He could hear Jill following him, the chains making a small clinking noise. He hesitated just inside the door and pointed for her to take a seat. She walked past him and began to buckle into the passenger area. He closed the door and strode forward, taking the pilot seat.

"You can fly one of these, right?"

"I can." He began turning on the engines and doing a preflight check.

"So, you're a pilot?"

"I'm much more."

Long seconds ticked by before she spoke again. "I'd really like a distraction from the crazy we're about to do. Can you tell me about yourself? I mean, we're in this together. I've told you things about me. Screwed over by Earth, how I was sold into slavery, and defended myself against a bug alien."

He buckled in. "Give me a moment." He checked the status of the cargo bay. It was clear of life signs, sealed, and he had been given access to depressurize. He did that next, then lifted the shuttle enough to fly out the now open exterior doors.

The dead moon was almost as black as space. *The Vorge* had flown behind it to hide from all traffic going to Flax Colony. He slowly put distance between the shuttle and the larger vessel, then picked up speed. He set course before speaking again.

"I'm Cavas Vellar, second born of the first litter of Beltsen Vellar. We are part of an old, very wealthy and powerful family on Tryleskian. That's our home planet. I hit adulthood and joined the military. I rose quickly in the ranks. I was the high commander, only one position down from the supreme commander. That's who controls the military."

He kept his attention on the scanners, not wanting to look at her. Guilt surfaced over being attracted to Jill. She'd gone through several traumas. The last thing she needed was a male feeling lust. They were there on a mission to find his younger brother, not for him to ogle her body.

"That sounds impressive."

He smiled at her uncertain tone. He also picked up a hint of nervousness still.

"I'm very skilled with combat and I'm a first-rate pilot. Not only shuttles. I can fly almost anything. Enemy vessels included." He paused. "I've led countless dangerous missions on alien worlds."

"That makes me feel better."

"Just follow my lead. I'm experienced at adjusting to situations to fit in with other cultures. Even the criminal element. I've gone undercover often to seek out and arrest dangerous enemies or rescue captives. Sometimes both at the same time."

"Have you ever had to play a slaver before?"

He hesitated. "No. I did, however, once pretend to be a pirate captain with a crew of murderers. They were my men, on a pirate vessel we commandeered. We had to go to a station that had been overtaken, kill those in charge, and free the four-hundred-plus hostages. That mission was successful."

"How many bad guys did you have to take out? How many of your men helped?"

He thought for a moment. "There were eight of us in total against seventy-six pirates."

She grew silent. He wasn't sure if that comforted her or not. He didn't have time to check. They were coming up on Flax Colony and some air traffic.

Cavas flew toward the surface. The shuttle vibrated once they reached the atmosphere, and he adjusted the gravity stabilizers to make it a smoother transition for his passenger. She wasn't used to space flight.

Once they were at two thousand feet and well below any monitoring devices from the colony, he changed course, flying even lower, heading away from it and toward their target. There was no certainty that Cavas was being held at the arena, but it was the most likely probability with the information they'd learned. It was a secure location, one he'd have chosen if he were Yorlian Trevis.

He needed to think like the enemy.

Chapter Five

Jill felt more afraid after the shuttle landed than when she'd first gotten aboard. They had arrived on Flax Colony. Her first trip to the planet had been against her will as a slave. The second time was by choice to play a role. It was time to put her game face on.

The big lion alien stood, striding toward her.

The outfit Cavas wore showed off his muscular body. The open front of the shirt proved his abs had abs. He had to be the most fit man ever. Cathian had also been really fit, but the blue-eyed brother had been thinner. He'd also worn baggy clothing that hid a lot of his shape.

Cavas's skin was tanned to a golden bronze and the thin white material over his bulging arms seemed at risk of splitting apart if he flexed his biceps. He paused before her, and his golden eyes peered into hers. They truly were striking and beautiful, in a predatory way. She hated noticing all of that about him. She felt bad for crushing a little on her alien savior. He'd shown no interest in her.

"Take some deep breaths." He wrinkled his nose. "You smell of fear."

His words and disgusted look killed any thoughts she might have of him feeling any chemistry between them. She unbuckled from the seat and carefully took hold of the long chain that was attached to the thick collar at her throat. It had a quick release on the back that her hair covered, unlike the last one she'd worn. As she stood, Jill once again felt small compared to Cavas. He towered over her by a good foot.

"Fear is normal. A slave would be afraid of her master."

"I'd never harm you."

"I know that. I just don't want to end up actually being a slave again or killed if we're caught."

He gave her a slight nod and spoke with a firm, reassuring voice. "We will be fine."

She hoped so. He got points for confidence. It was sexy. She tried to think of the important things she'd been told about slaves as she offered him the handle of the leash. Having wayward thoughts about him would only distract her from their mission. "Okay, slave lessons that I learned from Cia. Ready?"

"You have my full attention."

"I follow you, and I'm not allowed to speak until spoken to. When you stop, I stop behind you. When you take a seat, I sit at your feet. You're supposed to indicate to me where you want me. You never let go of my leash in public." She offered it to him again.

He hesitated but finally took it. A scowl confirmed his immense displeasure.

"I'm to do whatever you say immediately, without hesitation, or slaves are punished. Cia said it could be a strike with a fist or an open palm to the face, shoulders, back, or chest. Some masters are known to kick their slaves to make them fall."

Anger glinted in his eyes. "I won't be doing any of that."

"If I mess up and there's witnesses, strike me with your open palm on the back of my head. I'll pretend it hurts way more than it does. This is important, Cavas. Just avoid hitting the back of my neck if possible. This collar isn't the real deal. You might accidentally open the latch and make it fall off."

"I will *not* strike you." He appeared pissed.

She frowned up at him. "We both have roles to play if we want to pull this off." She waved her hand, gesturing to the length of him. "Master." She pointed at herself. "Slave. Cia was clear that masters are all vicious and mean. It will draw attention if you *don't* treat me like shit. I'm not saying I *want* you to hit me. I really don't. But I can take some slaps if it keeps anyone from arresting us. Got it?"

His mouth tightened and his golden eyes flashed annoyance. "We agree."

"Good. I won't take it personally. I promise. Cia also mentioned our master had a box in the arena, set up high. There's food present or brought to you. Our master liked his feet rubbed." She shuddered. "All four of them, apparently. There're trays of oils next to the chairs, and she said he'd bare his feet and indicate what oil he wanted his slave to rub with."

"I'm not having you massage my feet!"

She sighed. "We have to fit in, right? To act like we belong? From what she shared, that was one of the *least* horrific things that take place at the arena."

He sighed. "Do I even want to ask?"

"No. Most of it was degrading sex stuff."

He snarled before turning, walking toward the doors.

She rushed after him to avoid being choked by the chain. He opened the shuttle doors and the ramp automatically slid to the ground. The planet looked like a barren desert, with only that huge round structure next to the mountain. No other structures were in sight. Heat blasted inside the shuttle with the breeze.

Cavas walked forward, pulling out a small device from a hidden pocket in his pants. She followed. Once they were on the densely packed sand, he paused, pushed a button on the remote, and the ramp drew up, the doors on the shuttle closing and an electric-blue shell appeared to activate around the surface.

"Wow. Is that like a car alarm?"

"I don't know what a car alarm is. It's a shield. No one will be able to damage or enter the shuttle. Let's go. We've already drawn attention."

She hurried after him, which wasn't easy in her flimsy footwear. The sand was hot but not burning as her feet sank into the loose grains. Two armed guards were stationed in front of the large open doors leading into the tall arena behind them.

"Sir," one of the stated. "Name?"

"Garligon Press," Cavas huffed. "I was personally invited by Yorlian Trevis. He asked me to view his little *sport*. He's attempting to lure me into moving here." He grunted. "I'm not impressed so far. Yorl didn't tell you I was coming?"

"Um, no sir."

"That's an unforgivable insult," Cavas snarled. "Do you know who I am? I am one of the founding fifteen families on Tryleskian. I'm the firstborn of the first litter! I could easily buy a *hundred* dust planets larger than this one. Yorl should treat me better. I'm superior to him."

Jill was shocked—and suddenly glad to be standing close behind Cavas to prevent the guards from seeing that her mouth had dropped open. She snapped it closed. Cavas sounded like a mega-asshole, his tone haughty and scornful.

She tucked her chin lower, her gaze locked on the back of Cavas. That was slave protocol.

"Our humble apologies, sir. The communication must have been lost. Transmissions are unreliable this far from the colony." One of the guards backed up fast. "Allow me to lead you to a luxury box. This evening is a special event. There will be three fights tonight. Our most ferocious fighters will be presented. You were lucky to arrive when you did. Many city transports are due to arrive soon. It's a much-anticipated evening."

"Good," Cavas muttered. "It should be the best you have to offer. My time isn't to be wasted."

They were led inside and taken to a lift. It rose high before the doors opened. She followed behind Cavas, glancing to the side of the walkway they traversed. There were seats below for spectators, around the entire circular arena, and she got a good look at the center where the fights took place. The sight shocked her.

The deep pit of sand was expected—but the walls lining that pit were horrifying. They resembled metal, and there were sharp protruding objects covering almost every inch she could see. It would be suicide to attempt to climb out of that pit. The walls had to be at least twenty, maybe twenty-five feet high. There appeared to be razor wire that extended a few feet from the top of the walls. No one would be able to escape.

Cavas turned, and the motion tugged on her throat a little when he began to climb a set of steps. She tore her attention from the arena floor and focused on him. The stairs led to a sizable platform that had a back wall and a small roof to prevent the sun beating down on whoever was inside. A massive stone chair sat alone on the platform. Cushions had been placed along the back and seat.

Cavas stopped. "I was told there would be food," he grunted. "Did Yorl lie?"

"No, sir. I'll immediately have it sent."

"See that you do."

She inwardly flinched at how rude Cavas was being, but again, he was acting the part of a master. She'd told him herself how they behaved.

The guard hurried away, leaving them alone. Cavas turned to face her, his gaze moving over the arena.

"They've created a killing cage, only on a much larger scale."

She lifted her chin a little to glance surreptitiously at him. His words were spoken softly but the angry look on his face couldn't be missed. "I saw the walls that keep a fighter from trying to climb out."

"Those spikes aren't just to keep the prisoners from escaping. They're there to cause injury during a fight. A less-than-honorable male could throw his adversary into the walls. The spikes aren't long enough to be deadly but they'd cause massive blood loss that would severely cripple and give an unfair advantage. This kind of setup is banned on all worlds."

That news made Jill feel a little sick. "Who's the guy whose name you said, or did you just make it up?"

"Garligon Press is dead, but no one would know that. He and his entire family fled my home planet many years ago. Garligon would have been about fifteen at the time. They *were* one of the founding fifteen families. It would be impossible for most Tryleskians to identify them by sight. Their entire family kept to themselves in a remote region on my planet because they felt they were better than everyone else."

"How do you know he's dead?"

Cavas met her gaze. "I was part of the team that hunted their family cruiser. They were breaking every law imaginable, even after fleeing Tryleskian. His father refused to surrender, and he attacked our ships instead. We boarded. Garligon had murdered all seven of his slaves, four of his own children *born* of those slaves, and six military officers before he was taken down. I was the one who killed him."

"What if the guards contact him to verify who you are?"

He smiled. "The shuttle is sending out a signal blocker. Their communications from this area aren't getting to the colony."

"Smart."

Cavas turned, slowly, walking to the stone chair that was more like a throne. She followed, trying to digest what he'd just told her. No sympathy rose in her for the criminal. "Why did he kill his slaves and kids?"

"To prevent them from testifying against him when he was captured. As if their still warm bodies weren't enough for me to find him guilty. All

74

of them showed signs of long-term abuse. Including his own children. He deserved death."

She couldn't argue with that.

There was a long, wide step at the bottom of the throne-like chair. He turned and took a seat, and she lowered herself at his feet, adjusting her skirt to keep her modesty. It wasn't easy to do with so little material to work with. Her and Nara had managed to make a form of underwear, but it wasn't much more than a scrap of material to cover her slit.

"Four guards are on the walkway that leads to the mountain entrance."

She followed his gaze, keeping her head down. The pedestal-like box they were on sat higher, at the very top of the arena. It gave them an excellent view. The walkway on their level ran the entire circumference of the arena. Other luxury boxes were spaced out about thirty feet apart along the structure. The box to their left sat empty. Below, she could see a metal bridge that led from the arena to two massive open doors in the dark mountain. It had to be a good five hundred or so feet of distance from the arena to the doors. Four guards were patrolling the bridge—and they were heavily armed.

"That's not good."

"The level below must lead to that walkway to the mountain."

She agreed. The bridge looked like it sat one level down. "How are we going to get across that without being shot or captured?"

"I'm working on forming a plan."

She sealed her lips and turned her head. To their right was another box. That one *wasn't* empty. A big green toad alien sat on the rock throne, and he had two slaves at his feet. One resembled some type of pink bird. The other was of the same toad-looking race. Clearly a female, since she had large bumps on her chest. Jill easily counted four, since the slave didn't wear a top. Just a skirt at her rounded waist.

"Don't stare," Cavas whispered.

She dropped her gaze and faced his leg. Footsteps approached, and two new aliens came up the steps. They appeared male, and they resembled yellow humanoid lizards. They weren't very big. Maybe five feet tall, thin bodied, and they had thick tails. One carried a huge tray of food and a tall mug. The other had a smaller tray.

She tensed as they approached but they didn't touch her. One set down a tray next to her, the smaller one. The larger tray with food was placed on the opposite arm of Cavas's chair. They hurried away, tails dragging behind them.

"More spectators and guards are filling the arena. They must have sent a lot of transports from the colony. I'm estimating at least five hundred aliens filling those seats."

She darted a look. Cavas was right. The lower seats were being filled by various aliens and, as she lifted her gaze, she saw more masters arriving with female slaves to the other luxury boxes. Some guards stood on little platforms they used ladders to reach. All of them were armed with long weapons. It made her fear notch higher but none seemed to be paying them any attention.

"Eat your food," she suggested.

"I'm not hungry. Are you? There's plenty here."

"Don't you dare try to feed me," she warned. "That's a big no. Masters would never do that." She glanced at the small tray of colored liquids. "I should probably rub your feet."

"No."

She rolled her eyes. So much for Cavas playing along. She darted her gaze to the box next to them. The toad female was rubbing her master's leg with her head, kind of nuzzling him. He patted her bald head. The poor female bird alien held the toad master's foot in both hands and appeared to be licking his skin. Jill gagged a little but managed to muffle it, refusing to watch.

Cavas growled low, and she glanced up at him. He seemed to be staring at some of the other luxury boxes behind her, across the arena. She subtly tucked her head and peeked.

What she saw shocked her.

One gray rock-looking alien had a female blob thing giving him oral sex. The box next to them contained a furry rodent alien with another bird female. He had her on his lap, and from the way he was moving, they were definitely going at it.

She turned her head the other way and peeked again. It confirmed her suspicions. Most masters were having sex with their slaves. Some were screwing them, others were getting oral sex. Things had also heated up with toad alien and his two slaves. The toad female had her face buried in his lap. That wasn't something Jill really wanted to get a better look at.

She grit her teeth and glanced back up at Cavas.

His mouth had set in a grim line, his expression angry.

She swallowed hard and checked out the guards. They'd drawn attention, probably because theirs was the only luxury box where action *wasn't* taking place.

Panic filled her, and she rose to her feet, put her hands on Cavas's stomach and began to rub him. His skin was hot, smooth, and firm. He reached for her hands.

"Don't touch me."

"Go with it, damn it," she hissed. "The guards are watching us."

He tensed, his gaze widening as she slid her hands toward the waist of his pants. She lifted higher, trying to use her body to block the sight of his crotch. He grabbed her wrists.

"Stop."

"All the masters in the boxes are having sex," she whispered. "Are the guards still watching?"

He tore his gaze away from her and scanned around them stealthily, before grunting, "Yes."

"Then *act*, damn it. I am not getting arrested and sold again because you're a prude. We can totally fake getting it on."

He scowled but eased his hold on her wrists. She fumbled with his pants, staring into his golden eyes to avoid seeing what he had down there. He grimaced slightly as she tugged the material down to free his alien junk—and something thick and hard brushed against the side of her hand.

She froze for a moment, realizing Cavas had grown aroused. Alien or not, she figured that would be universal. Guys got turned-on when women touched their privates. Especially if those women were mostly naked—and that currently described her. The only alien penis she'd seen had been bug guy's, and that had been scary, strange, and a big *hell no*.

Cavas was much more attractive than bug alien in every way. Jill was tempted to take a peek to see what he was sporting down there. Instead, she lifted her leg and straddled his upper thighs, where material covered his skin. She trapped his freed cock between their bellies.

"What are you doing on my lap?" He ground out the words, looking enraged and dumbfounded at the same time. "I thought you'd just pretend to put your face close to me."

"Faking that we're fucking. Just go with it." She couldn't miss how his cock already felt larger and thicker against her bare belly, where she had their bodies pressed together to hide the fact he wasn't inside her. Jill started to lift her hips slightly and bounce on his lap.

"Grab my ass, Cavas," she softly urged. "Give them a show."

His big hands slid down her hips to wrap around her ass.

Awareness of how good it felt to be touched that way—by *Cavas*—jolted her entire body.

Jill tried hard to ignore the intimacy currently building between them. He'd shown no interest in her before that moment. His body was just responding to her touching him. It would be a mistake to think it was more than just a physical reaction on his part. She continued moving against him as if he were inside her. That thick length of his cock hardened even more, felt even bigger. Jill couldn't miss it.

Cavas was *hung*.

She made the mistake of staring into his eyes. The predatory look she'd seen before had returned. It was a reminder that he was probably dangerous as hell as he glared at her in a way that promised payback. His lips parted, and he flashed some sharp teeth when he bit his bottom lip.

She kept moving, more afraid of the guards than him.

"Stop!" he groaned, his hands tightening.

He was strong, and his hold on her became bruising. She had to stop moving or risk him clawing her ass when his sharp fingernails dug into her skin. He was breathing heavily.

"What's wrong?"

"I'm going to spill my seed all over us both if you don't hold still," he hissed, his teeth clenched.

She felt his cock twitch between them. "We were faking, remember? Pretending?"

"You climbed on me and rubbed against my dick with your bare skin," he pointed out wryly.

She felt his cock twitch again between their bodies. His his alien penis felt like a pipe. A hot and fleshy one, but still as hard and big as a steel pipe.

"Can you, um, make it go soft?"

A muscle in his jaw clenched as he ground his teeth, then his mouth parted and he took some deep breaths. "Just lean back, and I'll put myself away. You shouldn't have taken my dick out of my pants, Jill."

"I had to flash you at first to make it look real."

He released her ass and slid his hands between them. She was forced to lean back to give him room. He arched under her, easily lifting her entire body with his, and tucked that big boy away inside his pants. Then he shifted again, holding her in place as he seemed to adjust the angle of his hard-on into a more comfortable position.

She carefully eased off his lap—that's when she became aware of her own little issues.

Jill had been so busy acting, terrified that the guards would become suspicious of them, that she hadn't noticed how much she was responding to the feel of his hands on her ass, the friction of their bodies rubbing together. Her nipples ached, and there was a deep throbbing between her legs.

She inwardly cursed herself—but she would never admit Cavas had affected her so strongly. He was an alien. A lion man twice her size. She didn't even think he *liked* her. His body had simply responded to stimulus. It wasn't personal...but the way she was turned-on made her feel oddly guilty.

"The guards aren't staring at us anymore," he softly said.

"Good. My plan worked." She refused to look up at him as she spoke.

Chapter Six

Cavas shoved food into his mouth and chewed, a sad attempt to fill one need with another. He also tried to ignore the female at his feet. His dick pulsed, still filled with blood, and he began mentally replaying some of the most gruesome battles he'd ever fought.

It helped kill his lust for the human.

He couldn't even stay angry at Jill. The guards had taken notice of the two of them when males in the other boxes had begun to make use of their female slaves. It had angered him—until Jill had climbed onto his lap.

Then there had only been her.

She smelled good, her skin noticeably soft, and his body had responded despite him trying to ignore the silky skin caressing his dick.

He'd always seen the attractiveness of humans, but they were too frail and dainty to satisfy a Tryleskian male in bed.

His brother had fallen in love with Nara while in heat. Once his heart had been captured by her, he'd been left with no choice but to life-lock to the female. He'd partially pitied Cathian, certain that the sex would be dull. At least, he'd been a firm believer of that until Jill had practically attacked him.

The way she'd held on to him, vigorously grinding her hips, and the feel of her flesh against his dick had him reconsidering his previous stance.

His dick twitched again, and he quickly stopped thinking about Jill. It would be best if he tried hard to forget what she'd done. And how she'd made him feel. They were on a mission. It wasn't the time to be having those types of thoughts.

He focused on his surroundings and how to get inside the mountain. Retrieving Crath was his mission.

The spectators began to rumble, calling out loudly in different languages. He straightened in his seat, glad that his dick had finally softened. It made sitting easier.

Below, a large green beast stalked into view. A roar of rage came from the male. Cavas was certain it was the same alien from the cells under the bar.

He growled low, irritated that the male hadn't gotten away from his captors.

"What is it?"

"He was locked up where you were, inside the cells under the bar. It appears he wasn't able to escape if he's here...or they recaptured him."

A Kret came out next. Those aliens were a large race with bodies covered in thick scales and sharp appendages. It would be tough for the furry green beast to best one in battle, but not impossible.

He couldn't wait to have Yorlian Trevis arrested for his crimes. The two aliens in the arena were about to fight to the death to amuse onlookers.

"Get ready," he hissed. "We're going to wait for the fight to begin, and then head for the walkway. All attention will be focused on the battle."

"I think I should make a run for it, and you can chase me."

"No. I won't risk you."

"The guards are armed. Those weapons they're carrying can reach us from a distance if they shoot, right?"

"Yes."

"Right. That's bad. I still think it would look less suspicious if your slave made a run for it, and you had to chase me. It will get us close to that bridge. They'll be focused on me, not you. Then you can take them down."

"We'll move slow. They will probably believe I wanted to stretch my legs if they even notice we've left this box. The guards will wish to help me capture you if they think you're attempting an escape. I won't risk you getting hurt by them."

He glanced at Jill. Her delicate features were scrunched, and she didn't appear happy. Another roar gained his attention, and he stared down onto the arena floor. The green beast went after the Kret. The vicious alien dropped on all fours, presenting the thicker scales along its back, and rushed forward to meet the advancing green beast. They collided violently. The crowd cheered.

He darted a look at the guards. The fight kept their full attention, just as he assumed.

"Now," he urged, getting to his feet and grabbing her arm.

He pulled Jill up, dragging her toward the stairs. The small female kept up. If anyone noticed them on the move, he wasn't aware of it. A quick check on the guards had them still immersed in the battle taking place below.

The crowd yelled louder, seeming to chant for their favorite fighter. The green alien seemed to be winning.

They reached the lower platform, entering a covered corridor of sorts, and he moved faster, keeping hold of Jill's arm. A quick glance at the guards proved him right. They were all staring at the fight.

She stumbled a few times, her smaller body bumping into his at his side, where he kept her tucked against him, but he made sure she didn't trip. It was tempting to just toss her over his shoulder but she might get hurt if he had to drop her fast to free both arms to fight.

The space opened, and he saw the walkway and two of the guards to the right. There was a short hallway there that went under one of the luxury boxes. They both stiffened at the sight of him, turning their backs to the arena, where the noise had increased even more.

He released Jill's arm and dropped the stupid leash.

Cavas lunged forward, grabbing both guards by their throats. He lifted, using his momentum to propel him forward into the hallway, with both males until they hit the railing on the walkway on the other side, where it extended behind the arena. Cavas hoisted them higher and gave a mighty shove, throwing them toward the edge. As soon as their own weight began to pull them over, he released them.

Both went over, but if they yelled or screamed, it couldn't be heard over the deafening noise from the fight and the spectators inside the arena. Only someone in the luxury boxes could see them if they turned their heads away from the fight.

There had been four guards. The other two weren't in sight. He spun, ran to Jill where she waited inside the short hallway, and bent. She had those short legs, and they didn't have much time. He threw her over his shoulder, fisted the chain to prevent the leash from catching on anything, and then raced toward the mountain. The faster they could get out of the open and to the other side, the better.

Jill clutched at his back, but she didn't kick or struggle while lying over his shoulder. It wouldn't have mattered if she had. She wasn't a big female.

The double doors were open but the inside was dark. He ran into the mountain and made sure they were clear of possibly being hit by a laser blast from one of the arena guards before he gently dumped Jill back on her feet.

Cavas didn't have time to check on her. Instead, he quickly assessed the situation. There were overhead lights but they weren't on. Only sunlight came through the two exterior doors. There were cell-size containers with closed sides, backs and tops lining the walls, some two rows deep. Narrow paths ran between them. Prisoners were locked inside most of the ones he could see.

A male wearing a guard uniform walked around one of the cells, but he was looking at a data pad in his hand.

Cavas rushed forward silently and leapt, but the guard must have heard something, because he looked up right as Cavas crashed into him. He punched the surprised male hard in the face, breaking bone. The guard went limp under him, but he still breathed. A quick search found two weapons on the male. Cavas took them. He also found one of those bracelet keys for the locks, which he also swiped.

He rose up and noticed that he'd gained some attention from the prisoners. Cavas ignored them, storming back to Jill. She hugged her exposed waist, the chain wrapped around one of her arms, and she clutched the leash in her hand. He stared out into the sunshine and the metal walkway. No guards were rushing across it yet, coming to attack, but it was only a matter of time. The fight would end at some point and someone might notice the missing guards or them inside their viewing box.

He strode to the control panel next to the massive doors. It only took seconds to figure it out, and he began to flip switches, turning on the lights while sealing the mountain. Motors came to life and the heavy metal doors began to press together.

"What are you doing? You're locking us in here?" Jill's voice came out high-pitched.

"Yes. I have a plan."

"Do you want to share?"

"Not now."

She grumbled something he didn't catch. The doors met with a loud grinding of gears. There was probably a way for someone outside to open them again, but it would warn him of incoming enemies. It would also give him much-needed seconds to prepare a defense. He hurried to the first row of containers, peering inside.

"Crath?"

His brother wasn't inside. He walked behind them, looking into the other containers. His brother wasn't inside any that he passed.

Had he and Jill risked their lives for nothing?

He stomped across to the other containers, checking them all. He noticed there were a lot of blue aliens locked away, more so than any other color. Yorlian Trevis really *did* dislike them for whatever reason. It was just one more thing to detest about the criminal.

"Let us out!" a few of the prisoners demanded or begged.

"I'm looking for a Tryleskian. That's my race. Has anyone seen one? He'd be locked up, too."

A Parri slid his thick blue arm between the bars of his cell. It wasn't the same man from the prison under the drinking establishment. "There are two trainers of that race, but I saw a Tryleskian prisoner. Maybe that's who you're looking for? I'll tell you where he is if you let me go."

Cavas marched over to stand in front of the male's container. "Hair color?"

"Black."

That could be his brother. "Deal. Where did you see him?"

"Let me out and I'll show you."

Cavas eyed the lock but hesitated. "Don't betray me. I plan to let everyone out of here." He wasn't about to mention he planned to repeat what he'd done when he'd found those cells under the bar. The prisoners could rush out together first, and he'd escape while they provided a distraction. By closing the doors, he hoped it drew attention. That would mean the guards would gather on that walkway. Letting out the prisoners would mean they'd be the ones to confront them. That walkway would give the prisoners an advantage with close fighting quarters. They could lift and push the guards over the railings, making them fall to their deaths.

The Parri male glanced toward Jill, who'd crept closer.

"She's with me. No harm comes to her. Your word, Parri. You don't touch or go near her."

"Given," the male swore.

Cavas waved the bracelet and the lock popped open. The large blue male came out and pointed toward the back wall of the cavern. "There's a small opening there. They brought the Tryleskian prisoner in and took him that way. They haven't dragged him out to fight yet."

Cavas saw the scars on the male, including some healing injuries. "You were forced to fight?"

"Yes. I came here for engine parts and they arrested me, stole my shuttle, and brought me here. I didn't deserve any of this."

After everything he'd learned so far on Flax Colony, Cavas was willing to believe him. Most Parri he knew were good and honorable. "How many guards?"

"Usually just one or two during the fights. The trainers all left to watch. They'll be back soon." The Parri glanced at the closed doors. "We need to leave before it's over."

"Not yet. What's your name?"

"Nell." He glanced at Jill again, scowling.

"Don't look at her."

Nell met his gaze. "She's your slave?"

"No. She's a member of my team."

A quick show of relief flashed across the male's features. "Good. No one should own slaves."

"We agree." Cavas motioned for Jill and she moved to his side. He kept his body between her and the male, walking quickly toward where Nell had indicated his brother might be.

"Do I get a weapon?" she whispered.

"No." Cavas didn't want Jill to accidently shoot herself. She had no knowledge of alien weapons. He had both blasters in his pockets, within easy reach if he needed them.

They approached a smaller cavern with a few dim lights strung along the ceiling. He inched in front of Jill.

The first thing he saw in the much smaller space were boxes of supplies stacked about ten feet high. They made haphazard walls, blocking areas from his view. He moved around one and scanned the area. Six bunks were spaced apart, and there was a portable bathroom unit. It must be where the guards and trainers slept.

He gripped Jill's arm as he spun around, moving toward another blind spot. "Crath?"

There was a scuffling sound, but his younger littermate didn't call out. Cavas led Jill around another wall of stacked boxes and found a cage with bars on all sides. It contained a cot, and a small container with a lid for body waste.

A male stood locked inside.

Cavas grinned—he had never been happier to see his brother. "You idiot. How did you get yourself into this mess?"

Cavas released Jill and visually scanned Crath, taking in every detail. His brother had lost weight since the last time they'd seen each other. Bruises marred a few spots on his face and bared arms. Welts showed on his exposed chest. He wore only pants, ones that looked too big and needed washing. There were cuts on his feet but none seemed to be actively bleeding. The same for the scratches on his hands wrapped around the bars.

"Cavas?" Crath gawked at him, blinking rapidly. "What are you doing here?"

"Saving you." Cavas rushed to the lock and used the bracelet to free him. The door popped open, and Crath staggered out of the cage and right into his waiting arms.

Cavas hugged him tight, closing his eyes and ignoring the stench coming from his littermate. "You need a shower," he teased

"I'm aware. I need a lot of things." Crath wrapped his arms around him tight and squeezed.

His brother's hold wasn't overly firm. That alarmed Cavas. His brother might not be military, but he kept in amazing shape and took pride in his physical health. He and Crath tended to almost break bones when they embraced after long separations. The male he held trembled and barely had any strength.

Rage hit Cavas fast and hard for the ones responsible. "What did they do to you?"

Crath released him and they stared at each other. "Beatings. No food. I can't even tell you how long I've been here. I lost track of the days. Maybe a week? I'm just grateful to see you. Let's get out of here. I want

91

food, access to water, and clean clothes." He paused. "Tell me you have a military cruiser up there." He pointed toward the ceiling. "You need to send teams to overrun the colony to arrest most of the residents. Especially the ones running this planet. You'd be horrified over the crimes I've uncovered going on here. They must have figured out I was collecting evidence to show the authorities."

"That's not why you were locked up."

Crath frowned. "It must be. I thought I was careful, but I must have tipped them off. It's possible one of the Tryleskians living here recognized my face."

Cavas gripped his shoulders. "We don't have time to talk. I'll tell you everything later. Right now, we need to get out of here. Our escape depends on it."

"What do you mean escape? Of course your teams must be swarming the entire surface by now?"

Cavas understood why his brother would think so. He'd have brought a cruiser if he were still in the military. At least five hundred to a thousand soldiers would be under his command. They could easily take control of a colony and sort out the criminals from the victims.

"Crath, a cruiser isn't waiting. *The Vorge* is. We need to go."

Cavas turned away and snatched hold of Jill's hand, pulling her toward the door. Nell, the Parri, stood just outside, watching them. Cavas wasn't certain if he could trust the male, but he wasn't going to allow Jill out of his sight until they were safely back on the shuttle and off the planet.

"What do you mean?" Crath followed. "Cathian brought you?"

92

"This is not the time," Cavas snapped. "Right now, we need to focus on escaping."

Crath grunted. "Fine. Give me a weapon."

Cavas removed one from his pocket and tossed it over his shoulder. He smiled when he heard his brother catch it without issue. Crath couldn't be *too* hurt.

Then his amusement died. His brother would need that weapon to defend himself. He was in no shape for hand-to-hand battle.

Cavas strode to the center of the large cavern, visually checking the status of the guard. He still didn't move, out cold. "Listen to me," he bellowed. "I'm going to release all of you. Then we'll open those doors. We're going to have to fight our way out but there are plenty of transports outside. The colony brought a lot of spectators to the arena. It will be chaos once we leave here. Use the crowds to your advantage. Blend and mingle if you can. Do you understand? The large transports won't be heavily guarded but time isn't on our side."

He heard grumblings from some while other prisoners yelled their agreement.

Cavas gently pushed Jill toward his brother. "The female is with us. She's part of my team. I'm with the Tryleskian military. I've sent notifications to all local authorities of the atrocities being committed on Flax Colony. They are on their way."

He hated to lie, but he needed the prisoners motivated to escape. He *would* be sending evidence to the authorities, after he returned to *The Vorge*. "We don't have time to wait for the military to arrive. It's fight our way out or die. Who is with me?"

Now all the prisoners seemed onboard as they shouted in excitement. He glanced at Crath and whispered. "Keep the female at your side, wait for them to go first, and then we leave. Got it?"

"Yes." Crath frowned at Jill. "I know you."

"Not now," Cavas snapped. He strode away, quickly releasing the prisoners. There were over thirty of them. He had hoped for more, but it was the only plan they had.

He went to the door and activated it. The motors came on, and the prisoners gathered in front of the massive entrance, shifting restlessly.

As soon as the doors parted a few feet, they rushed forward, shoving and pushing each other.

Cavas pulled his blaster, getting in front of Jill and Crath. "Let's move! Stay behind me."

Chapter Seven

Jill ran after Cavas. The big alien's plan wasn't her favorite. It sounded nuts to her. Couldn't they have planned a second shuttle to pick them up on the walkway just outside the doors? Maybe brought some ropes to repel to the ground and then run for the shuttle?

No one had asked *her* though.

Both brothers had long legs, and she couldn't keep up as they ran full speed from the mountain. The bridge was at least clear of guards. The sounds in the arena were an indication that all hell had broken loose. There were screams and shouting. A strange boom sounded that she guessed might be from those long rifle weapons the guards carried.

They reached the other side, and both brothers disappeared inside the arena. Jill ran after them, panting, and someone slammed into her. She stumbled, hitting the wall hard enough to hurt. More bodies rushed past her. They were spectators who'd climbed to that level from the crowded seats below, fleeing for their lives. She hugged the wall, terrified of being trampled as more and more people appeared.

A toad alien glanced at her as he rushed by, then he spun around, making a grab for her, suction cups on the tips of his fingers. His big green tongue laved his wide, thin lips, and she hated the way he looked at her—lustily.

She wasn't about to allow him to kidnap or assault her in the chaos.

She had the chain in her hands. Jill fisting the handle and doubled the links, giving herself at a few feet to swing at him. She aimed for his face.

He jumped back, right into the path of other fleeing spectators. They knocked him against the railing, where he fought to not fall over the edge. Rage filled his gaze as he glared at her.

She tensed, prepared to use the chain to strangle him with if he came at her again.

Suddenly, a large hand grabbed her arm. She jerked her head, ready to swing the chain again…

It wasn't yet another strange alien, attempting to snag an unprotected slave.

Cavas snarled loudly enough for her to hear over the shouting and screams. He yanked her close and then lifted her, tossing her over his shoulder. It hurt but she wasn't about to complain.

She lost the grip on her leash and frantically reached for the back of her neck. With him running, her body slamming against his shoulder, it was tough to get ahold of the collar, but she managed. The latch disconnected and the collar fell off her throat. At least she no longer had to fear the chain snagging on something and breaking her neck at their present speed.

Bodies bumped into them but Cavas kept going, using the fleeing civilians as cover. She tried to peer around, searching for signs of Crath, but there were too many bodies. Someone from behind them slammed into her and she cried out.

Cavas held onto her legs tighter, then was running down steps. It almost made her pass out from the pain. She'd definitely have bruises where her hips were slamming against his broad shoulder. The only comfort was that it was probably just as tough on him to carry her and stay upright while attempting to get them outside.

"Almost there!" he yelled.

A boom sounded, and she twisted her head in time to watch as a purple alien's chest exploded. Purple blood splattered her, hitting her face, hair, and the exposed skin on her back and side.

Jill squeezed her eyes shut and grabbed hold of Cavas's waist. She was pretty sure that poor alien had been shot by one of the guards. It wasn't a prisoner she'd seen in the cavern.

That meant the guards were just aiming at anyone.

They were going to die.

Cavas kept moving, though, down more stairs. There were too many. They'd taken a lift to get that high, but either he couldn't reach it or the panicked crowd were blocking them.

Why had she volunteered to return to this planet? Jill wished she could go back in time to warn herself to avoid doing just that. Seeing that alien explode had been disgusting and horrifying. Human weapons were bad, but alien weapons were far worse if they could do *that* to a body.

Cavas suddenly released her legs and grabbed hold of her ass with one big hand. "Brace!"

She held her breath, tensing at his roared command. Jill was almost grateful she couldn't see what he could. Were they about to be shot? Die?

His body tightened under her, his muscles bunching—and then they were in the air. Her stomach rose to her throat in those frozen seconds, when she realized they were falling.

Then came the landing.

Cavas kind of hunched into a ball as his feet hit something hard enough that it knocked the air from her lungs as most of her body bounced off his back. Then he was pushing up, adjusting his hold on her, and running faster.

Something hit her face, sticking to her. She gasped in air and regretted it as sand hit her tongue, almost making her gag. But they were outside the arena.

When she heard his feet on metal, she forced her eyes open, glimpsing the ramp before everything went dark. Cavas spun around, almost making her puke with the fast action. She heard an engine roar to life.

"Get us out of here," Cavas panted.

"I'm working on it," Crath yelled. "The ramp is up. Grab on to something! They brought out the cannons and are aiming toward the landing field."

There was a loud boom outside that could be heard over the engines. Cavas twisted again, and her foot bumped something solid. Probably the shuttle wall. Then he dragged her down the front of his body and dropped down. She landed on top of him.

Jill opened her eyes, realizing they were on the shuttle floor. The engines roared louder, and it felt like they were shooting straight upward. It reminded her of the time she'd gone on a roller coaster. The force of the coaster had plastered her to the seat of the ride. Now, she was pressing tight against Cavas in the same way and couldn't push off.

The shuttle shook, tilting to one side sharply. The swift motion had her sliding off Cavas and slamming into the floor. Gravity pulled at her hard enough to hurt.

Cavas suddenly rolled on top of her, his big body pinning hers to the hard floor. He adjusted his arms, bracing somewhat to avoid crushing her.

She clutched at his shoulders in terror. "What's going on?"

"Rapid ascent to avoid being fired on, then I'm guessing they shot at us," he panted. "They missed, or we wouldn't be alive." Then he tore his gaze from hers, looking toward the pilot seats at the front of the shuttle. "Ease our speed slowly once you hit ten thousand feet. We'll be out of cannon range. Don't send us into the roof when you do. We're not belted in."

"I know what I'm doing!"

Cavas snarled at Crath. "You're a bad pilot."

Deep laughter came from the cockpit. "I got this big machine started and off the surface, didn't I? We're not blown apart."

Cavas growled and lowered his chin, staring into her eyes. Jill couldn't believe they were alive and in one piece. She ached a bit, would have a lot of bruises, but she could feel her limbs. They were all there. And it was kind of sweet, the way Cavas was pinning her down, trying to protect her. She managed a small smile.

His golden eyes narrowed. "What's amusing?"

"We did it."

He glanced at her hair and face, before taking a quick glance at her chest. "It's a good thing I know that blood isn't yours, or I'd assume you were critically injured. Are you hurt?"

"Banged up a bit, but I'll live."

The pressure eased from the swiftly moving shuttle and Cavas lifted off her, got to his feet, and then bent to clasp her wrists. He pulled her to her feet and turned them both, gently shoving her toward the nearest seat. "Belt in."

She watched him stride to the front of the shuttle and drop into the second pilot seat, where he strapped in.

"I'm taking over," Cavas demanded.

Crath lifted his hands high into the air. "All yours, brother. You did save my life. I'll let you pilot. Now tell me why you have Cathian's shuttle and vessel. Did you pull rank and take it over for one of your military missions? I bet he's furious."

Cavas turned in his seat and glanced at her with an expression Jill couldn't read. Then he turned back to his brother. "I resigned, Crath. Father asked Yorlian Trevis to arrest you and hold you prisoner."

"*What?* Why would he do that?"

Jill felt awful for Crath. He sounded beyond astonished. Earth had screwed her over, but Crath's own father had betrayed him. She closed her eyes, listening as Cavas explained everything...how he'd been ordered to board *The Vorge* with a team, take their cousin Raff, torture him to death, and how they'd ended up on the planet to rescue him, instead.

The engines grew quieter, and she could feel that they'd reached space. There was a queasy feeling during the transition. It passed quickly. Crath had also grown quiet. So had Cavas. Long minutes passed, and when Cavas finally spoke, it was to contact *The Vorge*.

"We have what we came for. Prepare medical. Our younger brother needs a checkup and to be healed of minor injuries."

She'd already learned to recognize some of the crew's voices. It was Cathian who answered. "And the female? Is she safe?"

"Jill is unharmed. She did great. I couldn't have done any of this without her assistance." Cavas stated.

His words made her proud, though all the uncertainty of living in space weighed heavily on her mind. There would be no returning to Earth. She had to find a way to survive, and that meant becoming a member of the crew. Regardless of what the other women on the ship had told her, nothing in life ever came free.

"Today was the first step in earning my keep," she whispered.

"What did you say, Jill?"

She opened her eyes, finding Cavas peering at her from the front. "Nothing. Just muttering to myself."

"We'll be back on *The Vorge* in minutes. I'll take Crath to medical. Do you need the android to run scans on you as well?"

"No. I'm good." She lowered her chin and stared at her arm, covered with purple blood. It was drying on her skin. There was more in her hair and along her back. "I definitely need a shower."

"I can't believe our father has gone this far..."

101

She looked up at Crath. His expression was filled with sadness as he stared at his brother. Cavas reached over and gripped his arm.

Jill blinked back tears, watching the silent exchange as one brother attempted to comfort the other. It made her miss having a family.

* * * * *

Cavas and Cathian got their youngest littermate settled into one of the crew cabins once the android had treated him. Most of Crath's injures were healed but he needed to regain his strength and some of his body mass. He'd lost a good twenty pounds in captivity. Crath had insisted on showering in the medical bay. Now he paced the living space, rubbing his wet mane.

"I can't believe Father would do this!"

Cavas shared a concerned look with Cathian. His older littermate started to speak, but Cavas was faster.

"We've known since he tried to hide Raff from our family and left him on Gluttren Four that he was capable of cruelty to his own blood relations."

Crath spun, staring at him. "I will never condone what he did, but a part of me hoped that Father believed Raff wasn't really from our bloodline. That he was protecting his younger littermate from an unknown female making a false claim of having his child. It was suspicious that only one Tryleskian infant would be born to that alien woman on Gluttren Four. I wanted to believe it was a horrible mistake on their parts, and that Father felt too much shame to admit he'd been wrong once Raff was located...but there's zero doubt that he's a Vellar."

"A couple of assassins went after Raff and his mother when our cousin was a child. Raff managed to kill them, and one of them carried proof that they were hired by our father. He discovered it on one of the bodies." Cathian said the words softly but with conviction.

Crath spun away, making a pained sound. "No one told me!"

"I only recently found out," Cathian admitted. "Raff isn't one to share much about his past. That's the evidence Raff has in his possession, and the reason Father ordered Cavas to bring a team to grab him. Raff threatened to expose that information if I was officially ordered to step down as ambassador, or if anyone tried to take *The Vorge* from me."

Crath shot a glare at Cavas. "You knew?"

"Cathian notified me because of Father's threats. He knew it would take the military to reclaim this vessel. I would have prevented any teams from being sent."

Crath began to pace again. "No one tells me anything!"

Cavas sighed. "You are difficult to speak to. The few messages I got from you were just that. Brief messages telling me where you were going next. This was sensitive information we wished to share with you, but not over unsecured communications. You're always off exploring different planets or going on adventures."

Crath snarled and threw himself down on the couch. "I search for injustices and report them. I do a lot more than you think!" He shot glares at both of his littermates. "I've worked undercover for the allied authorities for eight years."

Shock lashed at Cavas. He glanced at Cathian, seeing his surprise, too. "You didn't feel the need to tell us this?"

103

Crath sighed. "I work undercover. You don't share military secret missions with me, Cavas. You don't tell me what ambassador errands you're undertaking, Cathian. It was beneficial to have everyone believe I was traipsing to different places to escape my family responsibilities, spending the Vellar wealth. But I always let both of you know where I was going. On Flax Colony, I used my Brit identity, since there were so many Tryleskians living there. I didn't want to be abducted for ransom. That one previous attempt was more than enough."

"Does Father know you have this job?"

Crath met Cavas's gaze, shaking his head. "No. That was the point of working for the authorities. No one would suspect me. Father would have lectured me about my duty to family before aliens. He'd have demanded I live on our home planet to become law enforcement there instead. I didn't want that."

"You were sent to Flax Colony by the allied authorities?" Cavas wondered if that would cause them more problems in the future after what they'd done on the surface. They'd killed a few of Yorlian Trevis's employees while searching for Crath.

"Rumors were circulating about what was going on down there. Slaving. We had reports of visitors disappearing, never to be seen again. The few officers sent there disappeared. Command sent me, since I'm not their normal operative. The death fights and that arena were a complete surprise. It's far worse than we suspected. I need to send a report to my superiors. They'll have teams headed that way to clean it all out." Crath stood. "I need access to your bridge."

"Keep our family business out of your report," Cavas warned.

Crath approached him, narrowing his eyes. "Why? They should know what our father has done."

"We don't need their interference, or the attention to our name," Cathian growled.

"We'll handle Father ourselves. The other litters are aware of what he's done." Cavas stepped closer and leaned in until his forehead touched his younger littermate's. "We're protecting our position on Tryleskian. Father isn't going to take all of us down with him by shaming our name. Why do you think Raff hasn't come forward? The other founding families might rise against us and take everything away. Including Cathian's position as our home world's ambassador." He paused. *The Vorge* would be lost if all Vellar assets are taken."

Crath closed his eyes and remained pressed against him. When his eyes opened, his rage was clear. "You're right." He moved back and gazed at Cathian. "You've always been like a father figure to all the litters, more so than Beltsen Vellar ever was. We won't allow your ship to be taken." Then he peered deeply into Cavas's eyes. "I'm not becoming the head of our family. Are you going to step in to fill Father's position?"

Cavas snorted. "No. We'll leave that to the next litter to figure out. They are fully capable and extremely eager. I told Cathian to make them sign over ownership of this vessel as a thank you for stepping aside. The three of us would be miserable being politicians and playing nice with the other founding families."

Crath laughed. "Truth. What did they say?"

"They agree, as long as Cathian remains our home-world ambassador. He will. Once they have control of our holdings, the transfer of ownership will become their first priority."

Crath grew solemn. "I'm going to the bridge to make my report. I lost a shuttle down there. I'll tell them I called one of my brothers to get me since I knew *The Vorge* was in the area. That way, it explains why I'm contacting them from your bridge. All they need to know is what's really happening on Flax Colony."

The moment the doors closed behind their youngest littermate, Cathian sighed. "He seems to be doing well. Opinion?"

Cavas thought about it. "I agree. He surprised me, though. Did you have any idea he was working for the allied authorities? I didn't."

"Not a single hint."

"I think he's tougher than either of us imagined. It makes me angry that he never told us what he was really doing. I wish that he had." Cavas sighed. "I'm going to go check on Jill. She really did a good job down there."

Cathian smiled. "I've always told you that my crew is the best."

"You just got her today."

"And we're keeping her. The females have demanded that we do so. She also impressed me by offering to go with you. Jill should fit right in with our crew."

"You're just grateful it wasn't Nara down there with me."

Cathian chuckled. "True."

Chapter Eight

Jill felt a thousand times better after her shower. Food had been waiting on the table when she'd gotten out of the bathroom, indicating someone had been inside her cabin, but they hadn't left a note.

She had almost finished her meal when she heard a chime. She frowned, glancing around. It came again and she stood, going to the door.

It auto opened as she approached.

Cavas stood on the other side. His gaze ran down her body. "Did you find any injures?"

"Just some bruising."

"The android can speed the healing of them. I'd be happy to escort you."

"I'm fine. Does food magically appear on this ship, or is it normal for one of the crew to deliver meals to my table?"

He stepped forward suddenly, almost bumping into her. She moved back to avoid their bodies colliding. He inhaled deeply. "It was Midgel."

The doors sealed at his back, closing him inside the cabin with her. "How can you tell?"

He reached up and tapped his nose. "Her scent is faint but present. Nara probably asked her to do that after the day you've had. Did you feel like eating the evening meal with the crew?"

"That was nice of them. And no, I wasn't up for company."

"There's a food replicator in here." He stepped around her. "Did anyone show you how to use one?"

"No."

She followed him as he moved toward one of the walls that she guessed passed for a spaceship kitchen, since it had a sink and some cabinets she hadn't explored yet. There were also two weird-looking machines.

He pointed to the largest one. "This is the food replicator. It's easy to figure out, once you get the hang of it. Cathian has top-of-the-line ones, but they aren't stocked the way they should be, since they have Midgel aboard and they enjoy fresh-cooked meals. Food replicators are great for snacks and drinks, though. It's voice activated." He pointed to the other machine. "That is basically for trash. Put your used dishes inside and it breaks down the components for the replicator to make more when you want to eat."

He touched the food replicator. "Two cudda, cold." He dropped his hand, his gaze fixed on her. "Just touch and speak. It's easy."

There was a slight hum, and seconds later, two glasses slid down from the underside of the machine. They were filled with a red-tinted liquid. He lifted them, holding one out to her. "It's a celebratory drink. I always celebrate with my team after a successful mission."

She took the chilled drink. "Is it strong?"

He gave a nod. "Nara drinks it. She said one gives her a good feeling, but never drink more than three. I chose cudda because it's one of her favorites."

"Got it." She took a sip, smiling. "It tastes like a sweet wine!"

He took a bigger drink of his. "You did well today. Thank you."

"How is Crath?"

"He's doing surprisingly well. He'll quickly recover from his ordeal. Tryleskians are tough, and we do heal fast."

"I meant up here." She tapped her temple before taking another sip.

"He's highly disappointed by our father's actions yet again. We all are. He didn't wish to believe he was capable of being that dishonorable."

"Fathers can be assholes."

He arched an eyebrow.

"I told you what Earth is like. I never met mine, and I'm sure he never gave a second thought about leaving my mom pregnant after he walked away. That's how some men are. My mom was just sex to him. Fortunately, she could afford to keep me."

A muscle in his jaw flexed. "Was it forced?"

She shook her head. "She was curious about what it would be like to have sex, and she found an attractive man who was willing to do her for free. So—here I am. Really romantic, right?" She rolled her eyes. "Most of the guys on Earth who will have sex without payment are unattractive or such assholes no one would want to touch them...unless they're seriously desperate to have a child, or maybe to get treated better at work and paid more."

He quickly drank the contents of his glass, slamming it down. She startled, wary of his angry expression. His golden eyes were flashing predatory again.

"I do not like anything I've heard about the males from your planet. Offspring are a blessed gift and should be rejoiced when they are created. The concept of not caring about that infuriates me."

"So you stick around after you have sex, to make sure a woman doesn't get pregnant?"

"I'm a Tryleskian."

She arched her eyebrows. "What does that mean?"

"We have to go into heat to be fertile."

"Right. Nara mentioned something about that. I take it there are no little Cavas kids out there?"

He shook his head. "There are older widowed females from my planet who volunteer for high-ranking military officers, to share our heat cycles. They are past their breeding years. I've always turned to them."

She almost choked on her drink.

He studied her. "Why are your eyes wide and your mouth hanging open?"

"Sorry." She stopped gaping at him. "Most guys wouldn't admit to doing some old woman. That's all." Her gaze ran up and down his body. She wasn't going to mention he must have been super gentle. He could probably accidently break bones on an elderly woman.

He scowled. "They aren't old. They are *older*. There's a difference. Are all your females unappealing after their breeding years?"

She thought about that. "No. You're right. I've met some very pretty women in their fifties on Earth. I just didn't peg you as being drawn to cougars." A laugh escaped her. "It shouldn't come as a surprise, though. You look like you're part cat."

He tilted his head a little, not looking amused.

"Shit. I'm sorry if I've insulted you. I didn't mean to. Aliens are still new to me. I need to learn how to stop blurting out what I'm thinking. It's been a long day, and I'm tired. I probably remind you of some kind of animal from your planet."

"You don't."

"Well...that's good."

"I choose older females past their breeding years to avoid having to life-lock to one if she ends up accidentally carrying my litter."

"You have to *marry* a woman if you get her pregnant?"

"Yes. Those females are tested to make certain they aren't fertile, and then are introduced to high-ranking military members before the males go into heat. It's to make certain they are attracted to us."

She managed to keep her mouth from dropping open but she couldn't remain silent. "Mutual attraction is important, I guess."

"Not to a male in heat. But we want the females to be happy with the experience or they won't volunteer again. The military heavily depends on the widows to get us through our heat, since none of us are life-locked. Long-term service requires all our time. To have a family would diminish our dedication, since a family would come first."

"None of your high-ranking military personnel are married?"

"No. Our commitment to protect Tryleskian must be our top priority. Once a male life-locks, he may remain in service, but his duties are limited to what can be done while staying on our home planet."

"Is it the same for your women?"

He chuckled. "There are none in the military."

"That sounds sexist."

He gave her a confused look but it cleared quickly. "I believe I understand. Nara and I once had this discussion. Our females have no desire to fight or train. Nor do they wish to leave our home world, unless it's a short vacation. They are coddled and pampered. It's what they desire. I've never met one who wished for more. I would support one of my sisters if she wished to leave the planet or to take a job. None of them do. They find a male to life-lock with and desire only to raise their litters."

"What about once they grow too old to have more kids? Not the widows, but the ones still married?"

"They enjoy the litters of their litters by helping to care for them."

Jill considered that. "I bet they do have a lot of grandbabies, if your kind has multiple births."

"Yes. If grandbabies is an Earth term for the children of their children."

She nodded, then gestured toward the table. "Would you like to sit?"

He hesitated. "You've admitted you're tired. I only came to check on you and share a quick drink. I've done so."

"Right." She felt a little disappointed that he wasn't sticking around for long. Talking to Cavas distracted her from being in this strange place, alone. "Well...thanks for that. Cudda is good, and now I can have more if I want since you showed me how to work that machine." It sounded like a good idea the moment she said it. She deserved to get a bit drunk after everything she'd endured.

"Sleep well."

"You too."

He stepped around her and headed toward the door. He almost reached it when it chimed. A low growl came from him, and he advanced until he'd almost smacked right into the door.

It auto opened, revealing Crath.

They stared at each other for a few silent seconds.

Cavas spoke first. "That was fast. Are the authorities sending teams to the surface?"

"Yes. They are combining resources and should be able to coordinate a sweep in six or seven days. It's the best they could do, considering where Flax Colony is located."

"Understandable. Were you looking for me? I was on my way to my cabin after checking on Jill." He glanced back at her. "We'll leave you."

She opened her mouth to tell him goodnight, but Crath pushed past him, entering her cabin. "It *is* you! I'm very glad that you weren't caught with me when we fled together." A big grin curved his lips as he walked toward her.

"I *did* get caught. Cavas and Dovis found me."

"I'm going to hug you. I'm familiar with Earth customs. I'd say we're good friends, after what we've been through together. I was certain our guards might make meals of us. Weren't you?"

He gently wrapped his arms around her waist and tugged her into his tall, broad body. She hesitated before lifting her arms to pat him on the back awkwardly.

A snarl had them both startling. Crath let her go and turned his head. Jill took a step back, releasing him, too.

Cavas stood close to them now, glaring at his brother. "You shouldn't touch Jill that way. You also shouldn't be in her cabin." He grabbed Crath by the arm, hauling him toward the door. "Sleep well, Jill."

She watched open-mouthed as Crath almost tripped, but Cavas kept a tight hold of him. The doors closed behind them, leaving her alone.

Jill shook her head. "That was weird." Then she turned, deciding it was time to see if she could use the food replicator on her own. A few more drinks would help her sleep like a baby.

Crath tore out of Cavas's hold near the lift and got in his personal space. "What was that?"

"Jill is tired. She was just freed earlier today, then went on a mission with me to retrieve you. It might be a custom to embrace on Earth, but you aren't human. You shouldn't touch her. She needs time to learn how to trust us. An alien bought her to be his sex slave, and she suffered a beating before I'd found her. It's probably left her fearful of males."

His brother stared at him, crossing his arms, before saying, "*You* were visiting her."

"I was making sure she didn't incur any injuries earlier. Your piloting skills didn't make for a smooth takeoff. She was thrown around on the floor."

Crath scowled. "We lifted off, and we weren't brought down when they fired at the shuttle. Don't complain. I'm used to piloting a solo flyer. I had the same model that Raff used to own, before he had to abandon it on Gluttren Four. Cathian's shuttle is larger and tougher to fly. I would have been happy to let *you* pilot, but you threw the forcefield control at me before taking off."

"To get *Jill*."

"I would have gone back if I'd noticed she wasn't following. I'm thankful that you were able to find her." Crath grinned. "She's beautiful, isn't she?"

Cavas felt every muscle in his body tighten as he studied his younger littermate. "She's human."

"A *beautiful* human. I almost got her to my shuttle before Yorl's people realized we'd escaped." He grinned again. "I was looking forward to spending time with her in my solo flyer. She would have had to sit on my lap, in my arms."

Anger began to spread through Cavas. His brother had no idea that he resisted the urge to hit him as he kept talking.

"I've always imagined what it would feel like to touch one. I'm eager to find out exactly how much pleasure it brings, being with a human. I've looked for one ever since Cathian found Nara. Now I'll have my chance with Jill."

His hands were on Crath before Cavas even realized his control had snapped. He slammed his younger littermate against the wall, pinning him, and got in his face with a snarl.

"Stay away from Jill! She's been through enough without you wishing to use her body to curb your curiosity. Tell Cathian to drop you off at a brothel or pleasure house if you need amusement with a female. It won't be *her*."

"What is *wrong* with you? I want a life-lock."

The words acted like a punch to the chest. Cavas released Crath and backed off. "What?"

"Look at how happy Cathian and Raff are with humans." His brother rolled his shoulders as he growled low at him. "York and Dovis, too. I'm not dishonorable like our father. I'd never use other people for my selfish gain. I plan to win the human's heart and talk her into life-locking with me. Jill is beautiful, and it was lucky that I found her on Flax Colony. I've been searching for months for one of her kind."

Cavas shook his head, stunned. "But you don't want to live on our home world."

"I don't have to. Humans travel. Look at the ones on this ship. I'm having a family-size cruiser custom built. It will be completed within a year, with all the specifications I've ordered. It shall be comfortable, have plenty of room for our litters, but armed for battle. Only the best for my future family. I am more than aware that humans are targets. No one will be able to take away my life-lock or our young." He smiled, glancing toward Jill's door. "Now get out of my way. I have a female to impress."

"No!" Cavas lunged forward and put his hands on his brother again.

Crath's eyes widened. It was only an instant before he recovered and shoved Cavas back, breaking his hold. "You can't tell me 'no.' She's not yours. You just met her. I saw the logs while I was on the bridge. You haven't even known her for a full day! Get your own human if you've decided to find a life-lock, now that your military service is over. That one is going to be *mine*."

Cavas's mind flashed to Jill on his lap, touching him. He couldn't forget the feel and scent of her...

The rage he felt wasn't reasonable, it didn't make sense even to him. Yet he couldn't deny wanting to beat on Crath for speaking about Jill and the future he planned with her.

"Did you hear me, Cavas?" Crath growled. "You aren't taking my human."

That angered him more. "Jill is *not* yours."

They glared at each other.

Cavas calmed first. "I don't wish to fight with you. But...something happened between Jill and I." He wanted to be honest with his brother. "I feel strangely protective of her, and drawn to her. I won't simply step aside and allow you to life-lock to her."

"You just met her. What could have possibly happened?"

He hesitated, not wanting to share the details. It probably hadn't meant anything to Jill, he'd felt confused about his strong attraction to the female. "She had to pretend to be my sex slave to access the arena to reach you. We had to get a little...intimate."

"Did you put your dick inside her?" Crath hissed the words, looking ready to attack.

"No. But I know what her flesh feels like against it."

His younger littermate snarled ferociously. He spun away, pacing. A long minute passed before Crath turned, watching him with hooded eyes. "Did you taste her hormones? Kiss with mouths?"

"No."

"It doesn't matter to me then. I still want her."

His emotions were jumbled between the urge to punch Crath or roar his frustration. Cavas loved his brother, but he didn't want him to claim Jill.

"You had no plans to life-lock to a female while you were in the military. You said it was for *other* males. Your priority has always been your career. That human isn't a distraction to keep you occupied while you figure out what you will do with your life now." Crath shook his head. "I plan to life-lock to her. Stay away from Jill. She *will* become mine."

"I'm not certain of my future right now, but I do know I plan to stay with Cathian. He's already accepted me as part of his crew. And I gave up my career for Raff and *you*. It would be best for Jill to live with other females of her kind; they are already bonding as friends. That means she'll want to stay on *The Vorge*. I'll be here with her, while you will leave soon. That's what you always do. *Leave*."

"I'm not fighting with you, Cavas. I owe you my life, but I want a human to life-lock to. I also plan to stay aboard *The Vorge* for a while. I've decided to take a break from my job after what happened on Flax Colony. I had a lot of time to think about what was important while I wondered if I'd die down there. I want a family. My cruiser won't be finished for almost a year. I can't expect a human to live on a solo flyer until that time." He grunted. "If I'm able to get it back."

"I understand your desire to life-lock with a human. I now see their appeal. It just won't be with Jill."

Crath snarled. "You can't stop me!" He tried to move past him toward Jill's door.

Cavas blocked his path. "Don't make me knock you out, brother. I will. Leave her alone."

They glared at each other.

The lift down the hall opened and Raff rushed forward, immediately shoving between them and growling in warning. "I won't have you two fighting. The Pods contacted me and explained what was going on."

He shot a dirty look at Crath. "You're in no shape to fight until you recover, and you know it." Then he glared at Cavas. "She got you hard, and you can't stop thinking about what she'd taste like and feel like under you. Trust me, it's as good as you think it will be, if my experience with Lilly is any indication—but *both* of you are forgetting that she's been traumatized."

Raff stepped back. "The last thing that human needs is either of you fighting over her. Right now, she's in her cabin drinking too much cudda, thinking about her dead family—who she misses—and afraid she'll do something to cause trouble on our ship. Her main worry is being asked to leave since, she has nowhere to go."

Cavas was filled with guilt. He noticed the communication device in Raff's ear. "Are you in contact with the Pods right now?"

Raff gave a sharp nod. "With Two."

"Ask Two to scan Jill's mind, to learn if she's attracted to Crath or me." He held his brother's gaze. "We'll let the female decide. It should be *her* choice. That's fair. I'll back away if she chooses you." It would be tough to do, but he wouldn't force a female to spend time with him if she wasn't attracted.

Raff sighed. "Did you hear him?" He paused, listening. He softly growled. "Fine." He shot them both warning looks. "Don't move or make a sound." He strode to Jill's door, and used a hand to indicate they both should get out of view.

Cavas and Crath moved farther down the corridor, leaning against the wall out of sight when Jill opened the door.

"I wanted to check on you," Raff stated. "My Lilly worries. Do you need anything?"

"I'm good. Thank you."

"Did anyone teach you how to reach others on the ship if you need help?"

"No."

Cavas regretted that he hadn't done so.

"Just think at the Pods. You focus on them, and then project your thoughts as if you're talking directly to them. They'll hear you. That's faster than getting you a communication device right now. We'll give you one tomorrow and teach you how to use it. I'm sure Crath or Cavas will be happy to teach you anything you wish to learn, as well. How are you getting along with my cousins? They aren't bothering you, are they?"

"No, not at all."

Cavas felt relief upon hearing that.

"What do you think of them?"

Jill was silent for long seconds, before she hesitantly answered, "They're nice."

"Good. You are safe on this ship, Jill. All you need do is tell me or any of the other males if someone is making you uncomfortable, and it will be handled. We all want you to feel safe and happy living with us."

"I appreciate that."

"I'll leave you now. Sleep well, Jill." Raff backed off. "The computer will alert you in the morning to wake. Half an hour later, breakfast will be served in the dining hall if you wish to eat with the crew. Just speak aloud and ask the computer to show you the way. There are lights that will activate to lead you there. It will take time for you to memorize the layout of a vessel this large."

The door closed, and Raff approached the brothers. His expression wasn't a happy one. He grimaced, obviously listening to whatever Two said to him.

Cavas felt nervous of what the Pod would share with his cousin. What if Jill decided she liked Crath more? Could he step aside? It would be extremely difficult.

121

"I really didn't want to hear that," Raff sighed, speaking to Two. "Fine."

He glanced between them but settled on Crath. "The female feels indebted to you for trying to rescue her from your cages. That's why she went on the mission with your brother, to attempt to save you in return. She had no sexual thoughts about you. I'm sorry."

Then he addressed Cavas, holding his gaze. "She thinks you have a huge cock, from what she felt of it on the planet, and she thinks your body is 'smoking hot.' I'll assume that's good. She also thought about kissing you in the arena, but was afraid you feel no attraction to her, that it's only one sided on her part."

Cavas wanted to smile, barely managing to avoid doing just that when he saw his younger littermate's expression. Crath appeared devastated.

"I hate having family right now. And I *really* hate that Cathian is in bed, loving Nara. That's why the Pod contacted *me*," Raff sighed. "I'm sorry, Crath. You're hurting. But there are other humans. We'll find you one." Then he glanced at Cavas. "I worry that you don't have the ability to feel enough to make a human happy."

Cavas gasped, insulted. "You think that of me? *You*?"

His cousin stepped close, almost bumping into his body. "I may have been an assassin but I was very close to my mother. She taught me how to love. I grew up believing my life was better with her in it. I just had to kill a lot of people to keep her safe. Losing her made me cold for a long while, but I *always* knew that I could love. A human must become your main priority. Don't touch our new female unless you can commit to her and put her first. I'll hurt you myself until you beg for mercy if you change your mind after gaining her heart."

Raff turned and walked away. "I'm not coming back. Don't fight. It will just upset everyone." He got into the lift, and it closed behind him.

"This is why I rarely visit." Crath was the first to speak. "Between the Pods reading our minds and Raff being onboard, I worry about getting killed."

Cavas scowled at him. "No one would hurt you on this ship."

"The Pods have read my mind but never shared my thoughts. That could change. I've imagined what it would be like to get a couple of the humans into my bed. Knowing I've spilled seed while thinking of their females, naked, would get me tossed out an airlock by our cousin. Dovis would just rip off my dick. York and Cathian would leave me alive, but they'd break a lot of my bones."

Cavas shook his head, not surprised by his brother's confession. "I'm sorry about Jill...but I am highly drawn to her, Crath. I want to see if bonding to her is possible." Then he reached out and pulled his brother into his embrace. "I'll help you find another human. Don't spill your seed thinking about mine, though. I won't break your bones, but I *would* make you regret it."

Crath hugged him back and chuckled. "Just help me find a human."

"Recover first. You've lost too much weight."

"We need to deal with Father first. He's a threat to any females we care about."

Cavas nodded against him. "Yes, we do."

123

Chapter Nine

"First meal will be served in the dining hall in half an hour, Jillian."

Jill stared at the ceiling as the robotic voice made the announcement in her cabin. Her head throbbed a little as she sat up, pushing the bed covers down to her lap. The slight hangover had probably come from drinking three of the cudda drinks before going to sleep.

She scooted to the edge of the comfortable mattress and swung her legs over the side. Standing, she headed into the bathroom. It was a nice one, albeit a bit *too* fancy. Alien technology was something that would take a while to adjust to. She used the toilet that came out of the wall, and then stripped off the shirt she'd slept in, stepping into a spray of warm water.

The shower helped alleviate her headache and wake her more. She dressed in stretchy pants and an oversized shirt, wishing for undergarments. It was odd to not be wearing them. She'd ask Sara or Nara about that when she saw them next. The only shoes she had were the ones from playing a slave. She put them on and exited her cabin, coming to a halt, since she didn't remember how to get to the dining hall.

Raff had visited her last night, giving her advice on that very thing. "Um, computer?"

"How may I help you, Jillian?"

"It's just Jill, please. Can you light up the floor or whatever and show me where the dining hall is?"

"Of course, Jill."

Lights along the edges of the hallway lit up next to her and ran in the direction of the lift. She took a few steps before the next door down the hall opened. Cavas stepped out but didn't see her. She stopped, watching him reading his data pad as he walked toward the lift.

"Good morning," she called.

He turned. "Jill. You're awake."

"The computer woke me."

"How did you sleep?"

"Great. I had a few drinks before bed."

He lowered the pad and slowly approached. "You should have told me you planned to celebrate more. I would have stayed."

She debated for a few seconds before telling him the truth. "I got a bit drunk, figuring I'd sleep better. New place, new bed and all that. Otherwise, I may have not slept much at all."

"You're safe here."

"I logically get that, but it's going to take some time for it to sink in. You know?"

"I do. I'm right next door to you," he motioned to the room he'd just come from, "feel free to come to me if you need anything. Even if it's to talk or just to be with someone."

That was considerate. "Thank you. I don't want to bother you, though."

"I would always welcome your company." A sexy smile curved his lips. "Anytime."

She stared into his golden eyes. Was he giving her the green light? It was tough to tell. Maybe he was just being nice. It was going to take her time to figure out alien men…at least his kind.

"Are you going to the dining hall for first meal?"

"Yes. Is that what you call breakfast?"

He nodded, motioning for her to walk with him. She liked the way he smelled. He'd obviously taken a shower, because his mane was a little damp, and he wore form-fitting black pants with boots. His shirt was long-sleeved, a dark blue, and much better than his slaver outfit. She did miss seeing his mostly bared chest, though.

They entered the lift together. It was a short ride before it opened again. The hallway on that floor was a bit wider. A few doors down, one slid open at their approach and they entered the dining hall. No one had arrived yet. He led her to one of the tables, where she took a seat. He took the one next to her, placing his pad on the table.

"Would you like a drink?"

"Do they have anything like coffee?"

Midgel came out of a door at the back of the room. "I have it." She hurried to a machine and touched it. "One Rust. One claw."

The replicator hummed, two drinks appearing in big mugs. The small alien woman grabbed them, placing them down on their table. "Food will be in ten minutes." Then she fled.

"Rust and claw?" Jill leaned forward, peering at the dark substance in her mug.

"Not appealing Earth names? Rust is a warm energy drink. Claw is the same, but more bitter." He lifted his mug. "I've seen other humans drink rust."

She lifted the warm mug, took a sniff, and smiled. "It smells like coffee." She took a sip. "Tastes almost like it, too. To drink rust on Earth would be bad. It's a residue left on metal that has broken down due to exposure to dampness. It would make you really sick, if not kill you."

"Cathian will have removed anything that could have harmed a human from our food stores. It's the same word but different meanings."

"Got it." She took another sip before setting it down. "Seems we're early."

"I like to get here before the others to catch up." He glanced at his pad.

"Go ahead. We have devices like that on Earth. It's how we keep in touch with everyone, read the news, or find something to entertain us."

"What kind of entertainment?"

"Movies. Shows. Some people live stream their lives for others to watch."

He scowled. "Why would they do that?"

"To earn money. I watch one live stream of someone who travels a lot. It was the only way I was going to see other countries."

"You don't travel on your planet?"

"It's expensive. I never left the city I lived in until I was arrested and sold to aliens." She cringed. "I always dreamed of seeing new places...but that wasn't what I had in mind."

He reached over, surprising her by taking her hand in his much larger one. "You will get to see amazing, beautiful places now. Safely. I'll make sure of it."

She kept hold of his hand, smiling shyly. "That sounds nice."

"We might have to make a short visit to Tryleskian. You'll love seeing my home world. It's beautiful."

"Do you have a house there?"

He shook his head. "I always stayed at one of our family estates. We own many. My favorite is our North Coastal one. The fourth litter lives there year-round. Three of the four are females. My sisters spoil me a bit." He grinned. "You'll like them, and they will love you. I'll take you to meet them."

"Are they married?"

He nodded. "They are."

"And they all live together?"

"Yes. Some litters decide to share residences. The estates are large. They have their own private living areas. It's not like they share rooms, unless they wish to dine or spend time together."

"I guess they would have to have a ton of bedrooms with your people having so many children."

He chuckled. "To have many litters is a blessing."

"Not necessarily for your women. They must be always pregnant!"

"Only every three years, when males go into heat. Some life-locked couples decide to stop after a few litters. It depends on if they can afford to feed and house that many. We do have medication for our females to take, to avoid becoming fertile. I wish it were so easy for males. They've tried, but our seed is very resilient."

She quickly glanced up and down his body. "Your men are too masculine, huh? I believe that."

He chuckled and lightly squeezed her hand. "That sounds like a compliment."

"It is." She peered into his eyes before focusing on their hands. "Can I ask you something?"

"Ask anything."

"Why are you holding my hand?"

He hesitated before saying, "I like touching you. Do you want me to stop?"

"I'm just going to be blunt...okay?"

"Please do."

"I can't tell if you're just being nice to me because I'm a stray alien that you think needs emotional support, or if you're interested in me as a woman. Which is it?"

"I'm interested in you as a woman, Jill. Is that a problem?"

Her heart pounded, and she had to swallow. "Nope. I just like to be clear."

He smiled. "We're compatible, just so you know. I'll assume you're already aware of that, after speaking to Nara. She's also into being very blunt. When I go into heat, it won't be a problem. We're sexually compatible in all ways."

Jill was glad to be seated. "I'm not past my breeding years."

"I know." He leaned in closer, glancing at her lips. "I—"

The doors opened. Nara and Cathian entered, followed by York and Sara.

Frustration rose in Jill. She wanted to know what Cavas was about to say before the interruption. He what? Didn't care that he could get her pregnant? Had a plan to avoid it? When did he go into heat? Would it be soon? What exactly did that *mean*?

The couples grabbed drinks and sat down at the same table as them. Nara grinned. "Did you hear the news yet?"

Cavas scowled, staring at Cathian. "Is it about Father?"

"We haven't heard from Dax since informing him we found Crath and he's safe. I know they are moving against Father soon. He'll inform us when that's been handled. I expect it to take a few days." Cathian grinned. "It's about Raff and Lilly."

"Lilly isn't sick!" Nara squealed. "We have two pregnant mamas now! She's carrying a baby. I saw the scan myself. It's tiny but healthy!"

Cavas couldn't respond at first. "A baby? Just one?" He locked gazes with Cathian, confused. "Is that because Lilly is human? Can they only carry one?"

His older littermate shook his head. "Humans can carry litters. Raff's single birth is from his mother's bloodlines. He may appear all Tryleskian, but his breeding abilities aren't."

"How?" Cavas's confusion grew.

"He doesn't go into heat the way we do. He's always fertile. Do not ask him about it," Cathian warned. "It seemed to make him feel shame."

That bothered him. "It shouldn't. There's nothing wrong with inheriting traits from a mother. Raff's mother was another race. It's to be expected."

"He's way touchy about it," York whispered. "Like, punch-you-in-the-face-if-you-say-a-word touchy. Just grin and tell him congratulations."

"Of course." Cavas turned his head to see Jill's reaction.

She seemed lost in thought. He squeezed her hand, and she lifted her head, her gaze meeting his. He smiled. She gave him one back, but it didn't reach her eyes. He wondered what she was thinking. He'd love to ask, but didn't feel it was appropriate to do so with witnesses.

Midgel came out carrying plates. The female put them down and rushed back to the kitchen for more. Dovis and Mari entered next.

"Did you send a message to Marrow? I want her back." Cathian shot him a look.

Cavas knew his older brother was still irritated that he'd asked one of his crew to leave the ship. "I did that last evening. She's on her way back."

"Did she find a mate?"

He shook his head at Sara. "Not yet. It disappointed her that she didn't have more time. I offered her the use of my shuttle for longer, but she refused. All the males she met were disappointing to her."

"Damn," Nara muttered. "We were hopeful. She's been moping around since Raff found Lilly."

York laughed. "If he can find a mate, anyone should be able to. I've heard her say it a thousand times."

The doors opened again, and the Pods entered. Cavas watched Midgel serve everyone before taking a seat at another table. He had to release Jill's hand, missing the contact, once they began to eat. She had such soft skin.

Conversation flowed between the crew. The topic mostly revolved around the upcoming babies and if they could help Marrow find a mate.

"Is Raff and Lilly not joining us? Crath is missing, too." Cavas had thought they were just running late but the meal was almost over.

Cathian answered. "Lilly is experiencing morning sickness. It's normal for humans. Raff is keeping her in bed and tending to her."

"It was horrible for the weeks it lasted," Sara muttered. "Puking is not fun."

"I took good care of you." York leaned over and kissed her cheek.

Cavas envied the way they smiled at each other.

"You so did," Sara agreed.

"Crath has decided to stay in his cabin for a few days to recover." Cathian glanced at the Pods before holding Cavas's gaze. Then he darted a look at Jill, before they studied each other again.

He inwardly cringed. Crath was probably avoiding him and Jill, not wishing to see them together.

"Is he handling it well?"

His older littermate gave a nod. "He'll be fine. Once he's recovered, we're going to make sure he is happy."

Cavas understood. The crew wanted to find Marrow a mate so she wasn't lonely. They'd want to do the same for Crath. "I'll help with that."

"We all will." Cathian lifted his glass in a toast. "To good futures for us all."

After the meal ended, Cavas took Jill's hand again and led her back to the lift. At his door, he stopped. "Would you like to come in to talk? I think we should."

She bit her lip. "Yeah. Sure. We should."

He let her enter first, glad for his time in the military. His bed had been made and everything was in order. No female liked a messy male. He figured that had to be universal, regardless of the alien race.

Chapter Ten

Jill was alone with Cavas. His cabin was almost exactly like hers, only the color scheme was a little more masculine with darker colors. He waved for her to take a seat on his couch, dropped his data pad on a table, and walked to the food replicator.

"What would you like to drink?"

"Another rust would be great. I like coffee. It tastes very similar."

He ordered himself a claw, carried the mugs to the small table in front of the couch, and sat close to her. He turned, facing her more. "I would like to discuss us. I'm not like your father or other males on Earth. I'm not looking for something only physical with you. I *will* admit I never considered taking a life-lock—but then I met you."

Her mouth fell open. "Life-lock? As in *marriage*? We just met yesterday."

"I'm more than aware. I take it humans don't make quick decisions about that?"

"Um, no. It honestly never crossed my mind that I'd ever get married, until I was arrested and told that bullshit about becoming an alien's bride. Once they handed us over to the aliens, I realized we were lied to. Not brides—*slaves*."

"I would like for you to consider that commitment with *me* now."

She tried not to gape at him. "You want to marry me? Just like that?" She snapped her fingers. "We don't even know each other."

"That's not true. You're brave. Smart. Attractive. I like you, Jill. Do you know how the males in high-standing families on my world find life-locks?"

"You know I don't."

His expression turned grim. "I was the exception since I was in the military. Every time one of my brothers was about to go into heat, notification would be sent to other families who were considered suitable. The fathers would send information about the breeding history of their unattached daughters to ours. Beauty and the ability to have many litters takes precedence over everything else. The head of our family, my father, would chose anywhere from three to five of them to meet with my brothers. It's a short process, during which they only spend a few minutes together. Once a female is selected, the couple shares his heat, and if the breeding is successful, the life-lock ceremony happens immediately after verification that she's carrying his litter."

She hoped her disgust didn't show. Jill analyzed everything he'd said, carefully going over the details. "Are you about to go into heat?"

"No. This has nothing to do with my heat cycle. I've never agreed with how life-locks are chosen, or the timing of them. Cathian went into heat early, and his crew found Nara to feed him. Our father also sent Tryleskian breeding candidates he'd personally selected for my brother to meet him before his cycle ended. Cathian didn't want any of them. Just Nara.

"They didn't even realize until after his cycle ended that Nara had been implanted with a birth-control device. It's why she didn't get pregnant. He life-locked to her *despite* her not carrying his litter. Because she captured his heart. That device has since been removed. She will carry his litter next time he goes into heat. Our best scientists have determined how to make certain that happens."

One thing he'd just said really had her curious. "Nara fed Cathian? You can't lift your own spoon or fork to eat while in heat? Are you paralyzed or something? Or is it like a traditional thing for a woman to feed a man?"

He chuckled and got more comfortable on the couch. "Neither. We need to ingest female hormones to make our seed fertile. Nara and I discussed this, too. We are *not* something you call a 'vampire' on Earth. We go down on females to perform oral sex many times, gaining those needed hormones by arousing a female and getting her to climax."

That flat-out shocked her.

"For days," he added, grinning. "Nara enjoyed Cathian's heat immensely. You will enjoy mine when it happens."

Jill felt her cheeks heat, pretty sure she was blushing.

"I choose *you*, Jill. I hope you will consider becoming my life-lock. I plan to stay on *The Vorge*. This is my future. I'd like you to move into my cabin, or I could share yours. I believe we'd make an excellent match. It's a simple, painless medical procedure to become life-locked."

"What about love?" she blurted out. "What kind of medical procedure? What are you *talking* about?"

"I'm overwhelming you. I understand. How about if we start with our physical attraction? It's strong on both our parts. Come to bed with me. Let me show you what we could have together. Nara said your women like to test before marrying someone. That means having sex first to make

136

certain he's a pleasing lover? Do I have that saying right? Let me show you that I'll pass that test."

Her mouth hung open again. Cavas was excellent at shocking her.

He chuckled. "Have I been too forthcoming?"

She sealed her mouth and swallowed hard. "Maybe a little."

He leaned closer. "I'll show you what a feeding is..."

Her heart pounded inside her chest. "Now?" Her voice came out a bit squeaky. "Here?"

"Yes."

She didn't know what to say.

Cavas inched even closer and reached out, cupping her face. "Don't panic, Jill. We'll take things slow."

"Oh...good."

In the next instant, he kissed her.

So much for slow, she thought, before his tongue delved into her mouth. She could have shoved him away...but she didn't. Curiosity had her meeting his tongue with her own.

He was good at kissing. *Too* good.

She quickly lost the ability to think, instead just feeling. There was nothing but Cavas. His warm, strange-but-sexy textured tongue making love to hers.

His big hands were suddenly on her ribs, and he easily lifted her. Then she was reclining on the couch, leaning her elbows on the plush cushions beneath them, Cavas coming down over her.

He nudged her thighs with his leg, and she parted them. Cavas didn't hesitate to move his hips closer until she felt the hard, thick press of his trapped cock right against the seam of her pants. He slowly began to rock, causing her to moan. It felt incredible as he rubbed against her clit.

A growl came from him. Where before it was scary, now it was sexy. His kisses became even more passionate, like he couldn't get enough of her.

Jill totally understood. No one had ever made her as hot as he did. Maybe it was the danger factor that he was an alien. Or because he was so handsome. He also looked part animal, and there was a wildness to the way he touched her.

She clawed at his shirt, hating the feel of the material, wanting to touch his skin instead. Cavas kept kissing her, his mouth fused to hers, and increased the pressure and speed of his hips rocking between her thighs. She wrapped her legs around his waist and fell flatter onto her back, but she didn't even care if they ended up on the floor as long as he kept doing what he was doing.

She ground her pelvis against that hard, thick length, wishing they were naked. The need to come had her aching. He moved against her as if he were just as desperate to make it happen.

Things were happening too fast, they were still dressed, but Jill was lost to how he made her feel. She'd never been so turned on. What he was doing felt too good.

Then she was crying out, her body seizing, as the climax tore through her.

Cavas snarled when she stopped kissing him and tore his mouth from hers. Jill was panting, her body trembling, trying desperately to breathe.

Then her eyes flew open when he lifted off her, quickly scooped her into his arms, and rushed toward the bed. He put her down before tearing at her clothing.

She didn't protest as material ripped in his rush to get her naked. Part of her expected him to scratch her skin, but nothing hurt. He bared her easily, since she didn't have underclothing on.

Jill caught her breath…almost…until he yanked his shirt over his head, throwing it to the side.

He had an *amazing* body. All that golden skin, and so many muscles.

He reached for the front of his pants next. "I'm going to feed from you first before I'm inside you," he warned as he bent, shoving down his pants.

His voice came out more snarl than not. It should have scared her. Fear didn't surface. She felt too good after he'd made her come, too lethargic as she recovered.

He dropped to his knees next to the bed before she could get a look at him naked from the waist down.

Cavas gripped her knees and he yanked her closer to the edge of the mattress and his body. Jill gasped at his strength, but before she could say or do anything, he parted her thighs and buried his face against her sex.

His hot mouth latched onto her clit, and she moaned loudly as his tongue lashed at the already oversensitive bud.

"Oh fuck," she cried out, her hands instantly going to his head. Her fingers speared into his thick mane of hair, the urge to hold on to something strong. She'd never had a guy go down on her before. "Cavas," she gasped. "I need to..."

He snarled against her clit, creating vibrations. He went at her aggressively, his tongue merciless in its speed and that strange, wonderful texture. Jill was lost to the pleasure. It was near painful, too, but it hurt too good to ask him to stop.

She didn't even think it was possible to come twice in a row, but it happened.

The world seemed to explode inside her head as pleasure splintered through her body. She barely noticed when he pulled his mouth away, but she felt his weight press down as he moved on top of her. She managed to open her eyes, locking gazes with him.

He was beautiful. His eyes were golden, predatory again, and so sexy. She glanced at his mouth. It looked fuller than normal, a little swollen from what he'd just done, and he licked them with that tongue of his that she now knew could do such amazing things.

"So fucking delicious," he growled.

One of his hands hooked her leg, pulling it up against his hip. He pinned it there. She felt the thick, broad tip of his cock bump against her slit. He adjusted a tiny bit, and then he pushed forward slowly.

Her body took him in. She felt super wet, and it helped as he eased inside. It was a tight fit. He felt really big and super hard.

She realized she'd been gripping his shoulders, and she clung to him as he pushed inside her a little, withdrew a hair, before driving his hips forward to make her take more of him. Their gazes remained locked. His eyes narrowed to mere slits and a deep purr rumbled from him. His chest touching her bare breasts vibrated from the sound.

"I'm keeping you, Jill." He worked himself into her deeper, moving slowly.

Jill had to close her eyes. Her body was on sensory overload.

She'd always wondered what sex with someone else would feel like. Never in her wildest fantasies had she imagined it would be *this* amazing.

Every thrust had her in ecstasy. It only built as he picked up the pace. She felt taken, owned by him. Cavas filled her, had her pinned under him, and she *loved* it.

Her world exploded again, and she felt and heard him coming with her.

Cavas panted, trying to catch his breath. Jill had stolen it, along with his sanity. Her taste, touching her, and being inside her, it had all been beyond wonderous. He'd never felt so sated after being with a female. Now she was filled with his seed. He'd emptied into her deep, his dick still sheathed by her hot, wet sex.

Nothing had ever felt righter than what they'd just shared.

He stared at her lovely face as she peered up at him. A grin split his lips. "We're life-locking."

Her eyes widened.

"You're my female, Jill. What we just shared is unique. We are much more than compatible—I'd say we're explosive. Tell me that you are aware of it, too. Tell me that it was the best sexual encounter you have ever had. If it wasn't, I will do better next time, until I am certain. I'll *prove* that I'm the best for you."

"I...I don't have anything to compare it to."

He cocked his head, certain he'd misunderstood. "What?"

A lovely shade of pink spread through her cheeks. "I own sex toys. There was no pain since I, um, took care of that years ago, with a toy. It's like a fake penis. Manufactured. But that was my first time with a person. You know? As in...I've never had sex with someone before."

As she explained, Cavas felt stunned.

She'd never been with a male.

She'd only pleasured herself.

He was her *first*.

He grinned. "So that *was* your best sexual encounter." Cavas was thrilled to be her only male. "Life-lock to me, Jill."

She studied him, biting her lip.

He leaned in and kissed her. His dick stiffened and throbbed. He wanted her again.

He began to move slow, taking her. She moaned against his tongue and immediately wrapped around him.

He'd give her more pleasure, until she couldn't possibly deny him.

By the time he let her out of this bed, Jill would agree to become his.

It was a good plan, if he said so himself. Cathian and his other male crew members were correct in locking themselves to humans. They might be frail and small, but touching them was the best thing he'd ever

142

experienced. He also admired Jill's courage, her inner strength, and he just...really liked *her*.

He was keeping her. It was settled.

Chapter Eleven

Jill cried out Cavas's name, clawing at the bedding. He had her on her hands and knees, taking her from behind, his hands cupping her breasts.

Sweat soaked her body as she collapsed on the mattress, fighting to catch her breath.

He gently separated them and adjusted her on his messed-up bedding until she lay curled on her side.

Death by dick. It's a real thing. At least, she felt like it might be. Cavas had made love to her countless times.

"I'll be right back. I'm getting us food and drinks."

"I'm never going to walk again," she muttered.

"What was that?"

"Nothing." She was beyond tender. Cavas was seriously hung. He put her sex toys to shame. It took effort to find the strength to sit up, and she winced, definitely a little tender between her legs.

She watched him strut naked to the food replicator in his cabin. He had an amazing ass. *Everything* about him was amazing. She reached for the covers but then hesitated. He'd just tear it away. He liked to see her naked and had made that very clear.

He returned quickly with bowls piled high with meat and vegetables. Alien forks were stabbed into the mix. She accepted one, inhaling the scent. It smelled good enough to make her stomach respond. Those sounds had him chuckling as he placed his food on the bed and went back for drinks. He placed those onto the table next to them.

Jill dug into the food with gusto. The seasoned meat tasted like beef, like she'd had before. The veggies were purple and red, but they were good. The closest she could compare them to was cabbage and...maybe onion? Whatever it was, she wasn't going to complain. She was starving.

"Slow down, or you might not *keep* it down."

She arched her eyebrows at him but said nothing.

He grinned. "I got us chilled drinks this time to cool our bodies. It's an energy supplement that humans seem to like."

"Thank you." She put the bowl down and lifted a mug, gave it a sniff, and decided to try it. It was some kind of sweet juice, but he was right. It was cold. She took a bigger gulp.

"Are you ready to life-lock to me?"

She met his gaze and saw a gleam of humor in his eyes. "If I say no?"

He grinned. "I'll keep convincing you until you say yes."

"I don't think I could take it."

His heated golden gaze swept down her body, resting on her breasts for long seconds, before he took another bite of his food. He chewed, swallowed, and then licked his lips. "I'm prepared to persuade you more after we eat."

She decided he *was* trying to kill her by dick. It was a hell of a way to go. She might be sore, but it had been worth it. "I need to sleep first. And take a shower."

"I'll not allow you to put space between us, Jill." His golden gaze flashed predatorily. "We'll shower together before we sleep. When we wake, I'll continue to convince you to agree."

She was starting to know that look well. He meant what he was saying and wouldn't back down. "It's crazy to get married just because you're super-hot and have mad sex skills."

"I will take that as a compliment."

"I'm almost afraid to find out what you're like in heat if your sex drive is this strong now."

That caused him to laugh. "I will avoid entering you until the end of my heat, but expect my mouth to live between your thighs during most of my cycle."

Jill currently hated her body, since his raspy words caused her clit to throb and her nipples to harden. She was thinking about sex, and it didn't make her want to crawl away from him. Instead, she wanted to climb onto his lap.

She used to hear her aunt and cousin complain about how sex wasn't all that great. They'd either lied, or their husbands had been shit in bed. Cavas certainly wasn't. Even sore and exhausted, she was willing to go another round with him.

"Is this your big plan? Sex me up until I can't think?"

"Is it working?"

She shoved more food into her mouth, dropping her gaze. He was too handsome when he was being cute and playful. She knew he was teasing, but at the same time, he was deadly serious.

"What are you thinking about, Jill?"

She swallowed, took a sip of the drink, and then sighed, looking at him again. "You're crazy."

"Perhaps, when it comes to *you*. We're good together."

He'd convinced her body. By the fifth or sixth time he'd gotten her off, she felt addicted to him. Owned. Possessed. She hadn't even felt upset about it. That might have been because he'd fucked her brains out. Or at least close to it. Now that he wasn't kissing her, touching her, or inside her, it was easier to think.

"What are your concerns? I'll alleviate them."

A tiny bit of her resented that he seemed to be able to read her so easily. "I don't know. It's just so fast. We should date for a while before making a huge decision like that. This life-locking is for life, right?"

"Yes."

"See? Scary stuff right there."

"Why?"

She held his gaze. "What if we decide we don't like each other in, say, a year? What if you meet someone you want more than me? What if we fight all the time and end up hating each other? What if our cultural differences are too drastic?" She pointed at him. "Tryleskian." She turned the finger toward her chest. "Human."

He got off the bed, put his bowl on the table, and then took hers. That went on the table, too. He sat next to her, then surprised her by lifting her onto his lap. She liked it when he wrapped his arms around her, holding her.

"Jill," he rasped. "It will work. We're very compatible. Haven't I proven that?"

"In bed, we're great. What about *out* of it?"

He turned her head, cupping her face with his hand. The intense stare he gave her made her heart race. She loved his beautiful eyes, but they were a reminder that he was an alien.

"We'll make it work because we want it to. I can compromise. You can, too. We'll find a middle ground if we have a disagreement. You want to discuss culture? In mine, your happiness will become my priority. I'm nothing like Earth males. We've already established that's an excellent quality."

She laughed. "True."

He held out his hand. She hesitated, but then put her hand on his, and he clasped them tight.

"We'll be together. One unit. A team. You and I will face everything together."

She stared at their combined hands...and longing hit. It had been years since she'd lost her family, since she'd been totally on her own. Once they were gone, she'd had no one to depend on. To love. Friends were nice, but she'd barely had any. The ones she did have weren't that close to her. They'd been co-workers or neighbors she'd only chatted with in passing.

Cavas was offering to make a life with her.

She looked up at him, the longing deepening.

"I want to give you my heart, Jill. I want you to birth my future litters. To grow old together. We will be happy. I'll make certain of it. Agree. You will never regret it."

She wanted to say yes. He was just that damn convincing.

"I'll let you sleep before you answer. You look tired. But you're staying with me. I refuse to be parted from you after we've bonded."

She almost laughed. By bonded, he meant they'd had a lot of sex together. "I hope you don't snore."

He grinned. "I don't care if *you* do. I'm keeping you."

Then he lifted her off his lap and got out of bed. "Shower. Then sleep."

Jill got off the bed, wincing at the tenderness between her legs. She could walk easily enough, though. Cavas led her into the bathroom, where he turned on the water and gently steered her in first.

"I'll go change the bedding quickly. I won't be long."

She stood under the pounding water and closed her eyes. It was tempting to give in to the big sexy alien. She forced her eyes open and began to clean her hair and body. A few minutes later, Cavas joined her.

Jill got out first and dried off. He had remade the bed and pulled back the covers. She crawled in, yawning, and made her way to the center of the huge mattress. That way, whatever side he liked, she wouldn't be in his way.

The lights dimmed and the mattress dipped behind her. Cavas pulled her into his arms, spooning her to his front. His cock was stiff again, the guy seemed to live with constant hard-ons, but he adjusted it against the back of her thigh to avoid poking her.

The kiss he placed on her cheek surprised her in its chasteness.

"Sleep well, my Jill. I know I will. You're where you belong."

She yawned again and adjusted her arms, hugging the one he had in front of her chest. It was nice to be held, his warm body curled around her back. He didn't even seem to mind her damp hair.

"Sleep well, Cavas. I like that you cuddle."

He chuckled. "I always want to hold you close. That will never change."

"Probably because you're afraid I might sneak out once you're asleep."

His arm around her tightened. "Try it, and I'll lick you until you pass out."

She laughed. "You probably would."

"It's a vow."

"Now I'm almost tempted to try." Another yawn escaped her, and she closed her eyes. "Maybe after I take a nap."

Cavas fell asleep fast, but as tired as she was, Jill remained awake. It gave her time to think. It felt right, being with Cavas. She didn't know him well but she really liked what she'd learned so far. She could even admit she was falling hardcore for the big alien. He'd saved her life twice. Once from that cell, and again at the arena when she'd fallen behind. He'd come back for her.

Everything from her old life was gone. There'd be no returning to Earth. But she found that didn't even upset her. Life had just been a day-to-day struggle there after she'd lost her family. She'd hated her job, thanks to dodging her jerk of a boss's sexual crap until he'd touched her, trying to force her to blow him. That had been the final straw.

If she hadn't been arrested, and remained on her planet, she'd have had to beg for another job. They were scarce where she lived. She might have even been forced to take two or three part-time jobs since those were easier to come by. They also paid less than a full-time job.

She'd always had to worry about making enough money to keep a roof over her head and food in her belly. The thought of getting sick was a real fear. Meds were expensive. She'd had zero expectations of ever becoming a mother or having a man in her life. Then she'd been sold to aliens. Made into a slave. Had to fight off the nasty bug alien who'd tripped and fallen onto his hideous sculpture.

She shoved that memory aside, never wanting to relive it again. Cavas had come into her life. He might be crazy to want to marry her right away, but he was an alien. That meant they were different. She reminded herself that was a good thing. At least, *he* was.

Cavas was courageous. He'd become her hero for saving her life. He might be a bit pushy, but he was hot enough to get away with it. That thought made her smile.

The sex had been mind-blowing. Every single time. He made sure to get her off before he came. She added that to the growing list of reasons to say yes.

Suddenly, it hit her—she *wanted* to stay with him. Even if they'd just met.

The world she lived in now—well, ship—couldn't be more drastically different from her old life. Maybe it was time to ditch the old way of thinking and live in the now.

That was Cavas. He might be crazy, but it was the best kind.

She bit her lip, opening her eyes and caressing his arm. It felt right, being in his bed, being held by him…and why *shouldn't* she keep him? He was offering. Hell, he was willing to sex her to death to get her onboard with his plan.

"Decision made," she sighed aloud. Then she wiggled against him and turned. "Cavas?"

He woke easily, his golden eyes snapping open. "What's wrong?" He lifted his head, glancing around the room for any possible threat.

She reached up and caressed his cheek.

He met her gaze, a confused look on his handsome face.

"Yes."

He still appeared bewildered.

"Yes. I'll become your life-lock."

A slow, sleepy grin spread across his lips. "We'll have the procedure done first thing in the morning and Cathian can perform the ceremony."

"Procedure? You still haven't explained that."

"It's painless and quick. There's nothing to worry about. I would never allow anything to hurt you. Trust me."

She gave a nod. "I do." And she meant it.

He leaned in and kissed her. He had the best lips. Gentle but aggressive at the same time. Jill opened to him—then she just as quickly broke the kiss. "I so want you right now, but I need sleep. You've worn me out."

He chuckled. "I plan to do that often."

"I don't doubt it."

"Thank you, Jill. You won't regret accepting me."

"I believe you about that, too." She turned and allowed him to spoon her tightly in front of his body again.

She closed her eyes and smiled. Cavas could make her happy. She had faith they were both committed to making a relationship work. Another yawn hit her, and she finally drifted off.

Behind her, Cavas grinned. Jill was his.

He mentally focused on the Pods, informing them of what he'd need in the morning. He'd probably woken them, but he felt no regret. There was no way he was going to get out of bed and release his female to send those messages to his brothers or the crew. He'd make it up to the Pods later.

He needed to take Jill to medical first thing once they woke. His second heart would be implanted into her body. It wasn't an actual one, but it would always make her carry his scent, telling others they belonged together. Cathian and Nara had done it. His brother's human had been fine and healthy since they'd life-locked. Jill would be, too.

He'd also need a nice dress made for Jill. Humans had marriage ceremonies. He'd watched the one Raff had with Lilly, since they'd recorded it to send to her family on Earth. Cavas had been curious enough to want to see it.

A soft noise came from Jill as she slept, and he chuckled. Her little snores were cute. He kissed the top of her head and snuggled closer.

For a male who never wanted to life-lock, he couldn't wait to do it. That was all Jill's doing. She'd changed him inside and made him feel love. He was grateful to be able to give her all of himself.

Chapter Twelve

Jill kept touching her chest where she'd been cut open. There wasn't even a scar to show the small incision. It was the miracle that was alien technology. The robot medic had painlessly transferred a small gland-like organ from Cavas's chest and put it inside hers. It had been the size of a grape, with small veins that attached to her own. She hadn't asked too many questions except to make certain it wasn't going to make her sick or suddenly grow a beard.

It had kind of freaked her out. Not knowing all the details was better. For her.

Cavas had found it funny when she'd asked about growing hair on her chin. Then he'd patiently explained about scents, how his "second heart" would add something to her bloodstream, and at that point she'd tuned him out. She'd never liked anything to do with blood or what was going on inside the body. It all made her squeamish.

The bottom line: It wouldn't hurt her and it made him happy.

"Are you nervous?"

She jolted from her thoughts and glanced at Nara. "A little."

The other woman gave her a sympathetic smile. "I knew Cathian for a matter of days before I fell madly in love with him. I couldn't imagine life without him. I was ready to sign on for life." She paused. "I've never regretted it once. Did you know that I was married before?"

Jill shook her head.

"I came from a wealthy family. I was so flattered when a man swore he loved me. I believed him, and the idea of someone wanting to spend their life with me and have a family seemed like the ultimate dream. No stupid contracts to have kids. I didn't want to *pay* some guy to act like he cared about me. I wanted the real thing.

"Instead, he drained my accounts after the marriage and made an absolute fool out of me. He wanted what I had. Not me."

"I'm sorry that happened to you."

"Me too, but it's not shocking, is it? That's how a lot of Earth guys are these days. So many women, so little time, and lots of money to be taken if you're a good liar or a woman is desperately lonely. Like I was." Nara shrugged. "Cathian is completely different from any man I ever knew on Earth. I can't even compare them. Whatever your expectations of marriage are, up that by about a million, and expect to be loved like you've never dreamed. I know it's happening fast, that might be worrisome, but it's a whole other lifestyle out here in space. Jump in with both feet and enjoy it. Cavas is a damn good guy."

Jill studied her, seeing nothing but honesty in her eyes. She relaxed slightly. "I know. He *is* a great guy. I think I already love him more than I ever thought I could love anyone. The only downside is that he's a bit bossy."

Nara chuckled. "Alpha male alien types are hot though, aren't they?"

"Totally."

Nara stepped back and glanced down. "You look beautiful. Take a peek." She spun around and touched part of the wall. It changed from a solid color to a mirror.

Jill moved closer. The dress was off-white, something she'd have never worn, but it was pretty. Not an exact wedding dress, since she hadn't wanted something bulky and layered with heavy material. It reminded her of something women might wear at some upscale summer party. It flattered her curves where it hugged her waist and showed just enough cleavage to be sexy.

"I love it."

"I imprinted your medical scans, ran it through a database of dresses in the replicator, and it showed me what you'd look like in them. I loved this one best. Thank you for trusting me to outfit you for your ceremony."

Jill studied her image. "Should I put on makeup? Do you have any?"

"No. Here's another thing to learn about aliens." Nara winked. "They don't expect us to wear any of that stuff. Just being you is perfect. You don't hide freckles and stuff in space. It just makes you more attractive to have spots."

Jill laughed. "Got it."

The door chimed, and Nara rushed to it. Mari stood there, wearing a dark dress. "They're waiting. We don't want to be late." Her gaze locked on Jill, and she smirked. "Cavas sent Dovis with me in case you changed your mind. He's under orders to toss you over his shoulder and carry you to the bridge. Cavas is *that* nervous."

Dovis stepped behind her, coming into view. "Don't make me do it. He'd probably hit me for touching you, even though he ordered me to. Then again, he punches like a child." A grin softened his words.

Jill laughed. "Is that so?"

"We were only staging a fight at the time." Dovis flashed some scary teeth. "I'm certain jealousy would motivate your male to punch harder. Do you want me to find out?"

"No." Jill ran her hands down the dress and took a deep breath. "I'm ready to go on my own steam."

"Let's do this." Nara picked up some replicated flowers that she'd brought with her and handed them to Jill. "You're a beautiful bride."

"There's no, like, bloodletting or anything, right?" Jill still worried about what a wedding to an alien involved.

"You already accepted his second heart. That's it. Worst part is over."

"I'm not going to grow a beard, right? Cavas said no, but I think he'd lie about that. I sure would."

Nara laughed at Jill's question and lowered her voice as they walked toward the couple waiting at the open door of her cabin. "No, but I've noticed an increase in my sex drive. That might be due to the amazing sex, though. It kind of goes hand in hand."

Jill's nerves fired up again in the lift and all the way to the bridge as she followed Mari and Dovis. Nara stayed by her side in support. Right before they reached the bridge, Nara bumped her shoulder.

Jill met her gaze.

"We're going to be sisters. I've always wanted one."

Jill's heart softened. "Me too."

"Then let's get you married to my brother-in-law to make it official."

The entire crew waited on the bridge. The view out the front of the ship was of some moon they were near. It was lovely.

158

Cavas was the one who took her breath away, though. He wore a black uniform similar to what she'd seen on the crew, only a more formal version. He'd never looked more handsome.

Tears blinded her but she blinked them back. He was about to become her husband.

Cathian stood next to Cavas, wearing his official ambassador ensemble, sash included. She barely glanced at him as she made her way to Cavas. He grinned, his golden eyes taking in every inch of her.

"Beautiful," he rasped.

"I didn't have to carry her in," Dovis joked.

Cavas held out his hands. Jill passed her flowers back to Nara, who gladly took them and moved next to Cathian with a big smile on her face. Jill clasped Cavas's larger hands and, at that point, made sure to give a smile to each member of the crew. They'd all come, even Lilly and Raff. The Pods beamed at her. Even Midgel hovered in a corner. She didn't smile, but she did give Jill a little nod.

Crath winked at her.

"We are assembled here today to life-lock Cavas and Jill," Cathian began.

Jill stared deeply into Cavas's golden eyes as his brother said the ceremonial words. They weren't quite like a wedding on Earth, but they'd meshed some of them into it. She agreed to locking her life to Cavas's. He swore to care for, love, and protect her for all their lives.

Then he was kissing her. Jill wrapped her arms around his neck, Cavas lifting her a little off her feet since he was so tall. Then he grinned. "Forever."

"Forever," she repeated.

"No way!" a female voice suddenly gasped loudly.

They all turned. A woman in rumpled pants and a shirt had entered the bridge. Jill took in her tall height, her muscular body, and the fact that she had thin brown fur covering her skin. She was an attractive alien, but one she'd never seen before.

"Marrow!" Some of the crew rushed at the new alien, hugging her.

The alien woman grinned big, hugging them back. She eventually got herself free again and gawked at Jill, before glaring at Cavas. "You too? *You*, Cavas? Shit! I'm only gone for a few days and you life-lock yourself to some new human? How in the hell did that happen? Did I hit my head and I'm unconscious? Is this some weird injury dream?"

Jill stiffened, a sense of dread filling her stomach. She glanced between the two of them. Had they dated? Slept together?

Marrow, whoever she was, appeared upset over walking into the end of their wedding. Why hadn't Cavas mentioned if he'd been dating someone on the ship before meeting her?

Jill caught Cavas's attention. "Were you and her...um...?"

"No!" He appeared horrified. "No! I've never touched Marrow. We're friends only."

Jill felt a hundred times better.

Cavas grinned. "Meet Jill, Marrow." He pulled Jill close, hugging her to his side. "While you were flying my shuttle, I was finding an amazing female."

"Unbelievable!" Marrow threw up her hands.

Crath crossed the bridge, putting his arm around Marrow. "I know. She likes him for some strange reason. I don't get it, either."

Marrow turned and hugged him before making a fist and rubbing her knuckles in his mane, almost giving him a noogie. "You're alive. I'd kiss you but...yuck. I'm not that desperate."

Crath chuckled. "I'd be afraid to let you put your lips on mine. I have a feeling you'd bite."

"I totally do." Marrow grinned at him. "Glad you're alive, troublemaker. You're like the bratty brother I never wanted. It's good to see you."

"You're like the scary sister who'd beat me while I slept if given the chance," he snorted. "I'm glad to be here."

"Why did you seem so upset when you walked in?" Jill asked.

Marrow met her gaze. "Everyone is finding someone except for me. It sucks! But I'm glad Cavas found you."

"It does suck to be alone," Crath agreed. He smiled. "We've got to be next, Marrow. It's just down to the two of us."

"We'll help you each find someone to love." Nara grinned. "Crath wants a human. What about you, Marrow?"

"Anyone male who isn't a controlling asshole, but he has to be sexually appealing."

"I resemble that," Crath teased.

Marrow rolled her eyes. "You're totally a controlling asshole. You're just charming about it. I'll leave you to a human. They seem to like that kind of thing. I'd beat you often and make you cry."

Cavas suddenly scooped Jill into his arms. "We're leaving. Welcome back, Marrow. Please don't interrupt us for a few days while we bond." He carried her toward the doors.

The crew stepped out of their way, shouting out congratulations. Once they reached the lift, Cavas grinned down at her. "Thank you for agreeing to be mine."

"I have a feeling the pleasure is going to be all mine."

He chuckled. "All ours. Many times. You'll never regret this."

"I know." Jill had actually found love in space—with a hot alien.

* * * * *

"What in the hell else did I miss? I wasn't gone *that* long." Marrow glanced around at the crew.

Cathian smiled. "My brother fell in lust with a human, and now that his military career is over, her happiness is his new mission in life."

"He stole her from me," Crath sighed.

A few of the crew snorted and laughed.

Marrow eyed him. "He stole her?"

Crath rolled his eyes. "I saw her first, tried to rescue her, but we got caught. Cavas got her off the planet, then took her back there to find me, and I wasn't willing to get my ass handed to me in a fight for her. Mostly because," he glanced at the Pods, "*they* said she liked his dick better than mine."

"That's not how it happened," One stated.

Two spoke next. "Jill was sexually attracted to Cavas. Not you."

"Close enough. She saw his dick instead of mine, or it might have been a different outcome. I'm sticking with that story. It soothes my bruised ego." Crath winked. "He got her. I'm alone. That doesn't mean I'm giving up on finding a cute human to call my own."

"The most important information is that Beltsen Vellar has *disappeared*," Nara announced, grinning. "And by that, I mean his second litter of sons kidnapped his ass and forced him to step down as the head of their family."

Marrow's mouth fell open.

Cathian pulled Nara against him. "Our brothers have confined him in a safe, secure location."

"Like the prisoner he should be," Nara muttered.

Cathian nodded. "He won't be making more problems for us. They are stripping him of his power, taking over family holdings and accounts, and he will remain where he is until death. None of them had the heart to kill him because that would hurt our mother. She's agreed to live in guarded seclusion with him for the rest of their lives. Once she was informed of all his misdeeds, Mother was very upset. I don't envy the remaining years of his life."

"My biological father was taken to the same location," Raff continued. "Those two males can rot together, thinking about all their shitty deeds."

Marrow bit her lip, scowling. "What about your title?" she asked Cathian. "I mean, if you aren't the Tryleskian ambassador, we're all out of a job."

"*The Vorge* belongs to us." Cathian chuckled. "The first litter. Myself, Cavas, and Crath are owners. The official paperwork was received only an hour ago. No one can take it away from us. I'll still represent my planet, we'll get paid, but our home on this ship is secure, always."

"The love boat is ours!" Nara cried.

"It's a bad love boat." Crath jerked his thumb toward Marrow. "Her and I are still without someone to life-lock with." He glanced at the Pods and Midgel. "And you four don't want or need someone else to share your life with."

"Relax," Raff ordered. "I have a plan."

Crath arched his eyebrows. "That is somewhat frightening, but I'm brave. Tell me what is brewing in that assassin's brain of yours."

"We got a message while Cavas was on Flax Colony, saving your ass."

"I haven't agreed." Cathian shot his cousin a glare.

Raff ignored him. "Remember how we took down that slaver who wanted Sara?"

"As if we could ever forget Prince Azerba," York growled, pulling her closer to his body.

"The Relon authorities saved half a dozen females from a shuttle that had landed on their planet for emergency repairs. Once the crew was arrested for having slaves onboard, they were eager to give information to earn a lighter sentence for their crime. It seems they were taking the females to a huge auction when their thrusters failed."

Raff paused. "The Relons know we're very protective of humans, considering what we did for Sara. There was a second shuttle that *didn't* land needing repairs. The crew flipped on them, too, but by that time, they were out of reach of Relon. They verified that there was at least one human female on that other shuttle, heading for that auction. They gave us the location of where it will be held in the hope that we'd rescue those slaves."

Crath grinned.

"It's dangerous," Cathian warned.

"That does nothing to help my situation." Marrow sighed. "But I do love a good fight."

"Huge auction of slaves," Raff reminded her. "Many races. I found all the information I could about the auction. It's the biggest one they hold annually, bringing in the best stock of slaves. They not only sell females, but males for fighting and hard labor. Perhaps we could find *you* someone to rescue as well."

Marrow grinned. "I'm so in."

"Me too." Crath looked pleased.

"Did you hear me when I said it would be dangerous?" Cathian scowled.

"We *are* a sanctuary for humans," Sara reminded him.

"We're in," the crew all stated, one at a time.

Crath chuckled, rubbing his hands together. "I'm best at undercover work. I want to lead this team."

"Cavas would probably argue with you about that."

Crath winked at Cathian. "He owes me. He got Jill. I get the next human."

Up next…Crath

About the Author

NY Times and USA Today Bestselling Author

I'm a full-time wife, mother, and author. I've been lucky enough to have spent over two decades with the love of my life and look forward to many, many more years with Mr. Laurann. I'm addicted to iced coffee, the occasional candy bar (or two), and trying to get at least five hours of sleep at night.

I love to write all kinds of stories. I think the best part about writing is the fact that real life is always uncertain, always tossing things at us that we have no control over, but when writing you can make sure there's always a happy ending. I love that about being an author. My favorite part is when I sit down at my computer desk, put on my headphones to listen to loud music to block out everything around me, so I can create worlds in front of me.

For the most up to date information, please visit my website. www.LaurannDohner.com

www.ingramcontent.com/pod-product-compliance
Lightning Source LLC
Chambersburg PA
CBHW020256130626
46549CB00005B/2237